T0062845

Also by Phyllis Eickelberg

Bearly Hidden
Desperate Measures
Haunting Conclusions
Chasing Shadows

DEADLINES

Phyllis Eickelberg
and
Doris Minard

abbott press

Abbott Press books may be ordered through booksellers or by contacting:

Abbott Press
1663 Liberty Drive
Bloomington, IN 47403
www.abbottpress.com
Phone: 1-866-697-5310

ISBN: 978-1-4582-1801-8 (sc)
ISBN: 978-1-4582-1802-5 (e)

Library of Congress Control Number: 2014918426

Printed in the United States of America.

Abbott Press rev. date: 10/29/2014

PREFACE

Combine former Nancy Drew wanna-be writers with a few decades of time leading to retirement, and something has to happen.

Since a complete, unwritten story had yet to be thought up, it was determined that one writer would be responsible for even-numbered chapters and the other, the odd-numbered chapters.

Starting with that premise, writer number one set the stage and took the protagonist to the edge of the proverbial cliff. Writer number two saved the protagonist and carefully walked her to a train track and a fast-moving train.

Back and forth went the protagonist, from one problem to another, but always, like Nancy Drew, saved at the last minute. It was a fun experience for both writers, who, after a while, couldn't tell who wrote what.

For other would-be writers, we suggest you get a friend and give the system a try. If nothing else, you'll have a grand time, and who knows where your story may end up.

ACKNOWLEDGEMENTS

The authors wish to express a special debt of gratitude to their patient spouses: Jim Eickelberg and Eugene Minard.

Thanks, too, to proofreaders and consultants Peter Saunders, Sam Hall, Carolyn Hegstad, Frank Yates, Anne Chaimov, Peter and Mariana Burke, Dinaz Rogers, Jason Schindler, Dennis Stillwagon, John and Kathe Burk, Patricia Fordney, Kay Ohara, Mary Waters, Teri Heitzman, and Joan Bostrom.

And thanks to special helpers known as the '49-ers; a group that had a lot to do with critiquing and hardly anything to do with gold mining or football.

CHAPTER

1

She's planning to kill him! I'm sure of it! Teddy Sanderson, Whittington's newest Girl Friday, hurried down the path knifing through the city park. She'd just uncovered what looked like the first step in a plot to murder a family friend. If she hurried, she could alert William Smith to his danger before he headed home for the day. A sudden gust of October wind lifted the edges of Teddy's thin red raincoat, and she clutched her armload of packages tighter. Spying an empty bench, she stopped to rearrange things. She stuffed a box of business cards into her black tote, and smiled. *New cards, new job, new me.* She scooped up the rest of her purchases and once more headed for her new office in the Stettler Building.

###

Across the street from the park, on the fifth floor of the Stettler, a pair of binoculars rested against the tired eyes of a man in his forties. He wore a business suit minus the jacket he'd draped over a chair. Sam Morgan heaved a sigh as he sipped coffee. He'd been watching the city park's north entrance since sunrise. If the tip he received was valid, he'd soon make headway with one of his more challenging assignments.

Cup to his lips, he paused. A man he knew only by the code name *Mario,* was approaching the park's north entrance. He had entered the

1

country as a student and affiliated himself with a radical environmentalist group passionate about animal rights. They called themselves the Delphi Alliance. In the years since they'd formed, they'd caused millions of dollars of damage to businesses around the country.

Sam stayed focused on the tall figure, excitedly whispering, "Come on! Come on!" He watched Mario enter the park, and then pause to reach in a pocket. With a thud, Sam's coffee cup landed on a nearby desk. It was replaced by a section of newspaper Sam grabbed as he bolted from his office.

Mario stood inside the park's north entrance, hands deep in the pockets of a worn leather jacket. Thick black eyebrows were pinched together in a frown, his pursed lips barely visible above a neatly trimmed beard. For a moment he watched a slim young woman hurrying toward him, struggling to control an armload of packages. No matter. Soon she would be gone.

Benches bordered both sides of the park's pathway with those on the west side chained to tall black garbage cans. Mario smiled, noting a section of the path splashed with white paint, then streaked with red. To members of the Delphi Alliance, white represented success, while red slashes reminded them of their pledge to disrupt this country's economy as *pay back* for perceived wrongs. He glanced at his Rolex. It was almost time for today's important exchange.

He walked toward the garbage can, pulling a brown paper bag from his pocket. He folded the bag to hide its white streaks, then placed it on top of the debris in the can. When it teetered on the edge, he pushed it down. Finally satisfied it wouldn't fall he walked to the bench on the opposite side of the path and settled next to an abandoned newspaper. He was thinking of Isaac, a compulsive worrier who often put Alliance members at risk. Today's exchange of information could have been accomplished far easier and with less risk than the plan Isaac set in motion.

A cool breeze ruffled the pages of the newspaper, and Mario picked it up. The headlines gave examples of government policies that Alliance members disagreed with. It was obviously time for them to plan another protest.

At the sound of high heels clicking on the path, Mario looked up, surprised at how quickly the blond woman with packages approached. As she passed, he ducked his head into the newspaper and watched her join people at the boulevard, waiting for pedestrian lights to change.

Mario checked his watch before glancing over his shoulder. A runner in black was approaching the park's south entrance. Mario stood, lifting his arms high overhead as if stretching. After a moment, he lowered his arms and joined the pedestrians waiting for the traffic signal to change.

To the right of the waiting group, Sam Morgan, brown eyes brimming with excitement, crossed the boulevard mid-block. The newspaper he'd grabbed as he left his office was still in his hands. *What a break*, he thought, ignoring a horn blast as he skillfully dodged cars. *If it hadn't been for Gwen's parolee, I'd never have known about this drop site.*

Intercepting a drop between groups of extremists was an adrenalin rush Sam had never been able to explain. He laughed. After today the Alliance would be in deep trouble and that pleased him. They were desperately naïve in choosing the park as a drop site.

By the time the traffic light changed and waiting pedestrians began crossing, Sam had reached the garbage can where Mario paused. He dropped his newspaper on the debris, then scooped part of it back up, pulling the white-streaked bag into the newspaper. With it tucked under his arm, he joined stragglers still crossing the street. Intercepting this information was almost like taking candy from a baby.

The runner whose code name was *Adam* had spotted Sam at the drop site, but he couldn't see what took place. His breathing had become ragged by the time he reached the garbage can and began looking for the package with white streaks. Frantically he searched, allowing newspapers and cans to tumble to the ground. One last sweep yielded nothing. The package wasn't there. The Alliance's schedule of plans for West Coast organizations was gone and he would be blamed.

Adam looked toward the boulevard and the pedestrians who had just crossed it. Sweat rolled down his face and his chest heaved. The package had to be with the man who paused at this location. Adam wiped debris from his hands and rushed across the street, ignoring the red light and blaring horns.

Sam glanced at mirrored reflections in store windows as he hurried. They showed a man sprinting across the street against the light. Was he the pickup man? Sam was almost running when he merged with a group of pedestrians. There was safety in numbers and the Stettler lobby was close.

Strolling shoppers forced the runner to slow his pace, but he kept the well-dressed man with the newspaper in sight. Adam wiped sweat from his forehead before plunging his hand into a pocket. His weapon was ready to use if necessary. He pushed through the shoppers, drawing closer to the man with the newspaper.

Sam knew he was in a tight spot. Ahead was the man called Mario, and behind, stalking him, came the pickup man. Sam broke into a run, his heart pounding. The combination of excitement tinged with fear was what kept him in this job. Like others in his field, he was an adrenalin junkie.

The pedestrians shifted, allowing Sam to surge ahead, but as he did, a sharp sting hit the back of his neck. He faltered, swatting at the stinging spot, dislodging something sharp and small. A light-headed feeling began sweeping over him. He was shutting down. He could feel it. Better to destroy the parcel than let the extremists regain control.

He could see the entrance to the Stettler Building ahead, but it seemed to recede as he struggled to reach it. At that moment he noticed a black bag of some kind, dangling from the arm of a pedestrian. The bag swung open with each step the woman took.

Focusing on the bag, Sam caught up to it and with his body shielding his actions he shoved the brown bag's contents into the gaping tote. As he completed the task, he stumbled.

The sudden jostle at the woman's side caused her to clutch her packages tighter. She looked toward the unsteady man beside her, and their eyes met. He took one more faltering step, and then fell.

CHAPTER

2

"Hey, man. Are you all right? Do you need help?" A long-legged youth with unkempt red hair bent over the figure sprawled on the sidewalk.

Teddy set her packages on the pavement and knelt, checking the fallen man's wrist for a pulse. "Is anyone a doctor?" she called. When no one stepped forward she shouted, "Call 9-1-1."

"Is he breathing?" asked the young man kneeling beside the victim. Thick lenses made his eyes seem too large for his face.

Teddy felt for a pulse at the man's throat. It was almost undetectable.

At her touch, the man's eyelids fluttered and his eyes moved over images close by. They came to rest on the woman. "T-Teddy?" He whispered the name through lips that didn't move. "Take…." His eyes rolled back, and slowly closed.

"What did you say?" Teddy caught her breath and leaned closer. "Repeat what you said." *Had he actually whispered her name?* She turned to the young man with thick lenses. "Did you hear what he said?"

"I don't think he's able to talk." The Good Samaritan raised the man's chin. "His airway's clear, but we're losing him. If you know CPR, we'd better get started."

Teddy nodded and placed her trembling hands in the center of the inert chest. She began pushing hard and fast.

###

Curious onlookers spilled into the street, pushing to see what was happening. Impatient drivers honked. Noise and confusion were escalating.

Mario glanced behind him. On the far side of a growing crowd was his friend Adam. He seemed to be pushing into a group clustered around something or someone.

As if connected by an invisible signal, Adam looked up. The panic on his face was unmistakable. He shook his head, nodding toward the milling pedestrians.

Mario retraced his steps, elbowing through the onlookers. The blond woman from the park and a redheaded man were kneeling beside a man sprawled on the sidewalk. Mario squeezed down next to Teddy.

"What happened?" he asked. "Did a car hit him?"

"He just collapsed. Are you a doctor?" Teddy glanced at the bearded stranger as she continued pushing hard and fast.

Mario shook his head and addressed the crowd. "Did anyone see what happened?"

No one responded, but the expression on Adam's face confirmed Mario's suspicions. Adam was somehow responsible, and that could mean only one thing—he didn't have the important package he was to have picked up. Mario turned to the woman doing chest compressions and whispered, "I am a special agent." To back up his claim he reached into his pocket and pulled out a badge that he flashed and put away.

Teddy heaved a sigh and nodded to the redheaded man. He immediately took over compressions. "Can you take a turn?" she asked the special agent.

"No. I cannot." Mario reached behind him to glance through packages Teddy had placed on the sidewalk. Nothing. No Alliance plans. He stood and walked around the woman, kneeling at her other side. Newspapers were scattered nearby. On closer inspection a lunch bag with white streaks was visible near the papers. Mario breathed a sigh. Somehow the fallen man had ended up with the package meant for Adam, and Adam had taken the appropriate steps to stop him.

Mario reached for the crumpled bag and plunged his hand inside. His jaw tightened. Nothing! Empty! He looked again at Adam and shook his head. With one quick movement, he slipped his hand into one of the fallen man's pockets.

"Stop! What are you doing?" Teddy elbowed the bearded man away. His actions seemed bizarre.

"I am checking for identification with medical conditions," he replied. "I am looking for a notice." He picked up a slack wrist with a wristwatch, but no medic alert bracelet.

Teddy continued watching him. His search through the victim's pockets produced a credit card and loose change. "Nothing," he mumbled, returning the possessions to the man's pockets. "There are no medicals to explain why this man fell."

"The police are here," a bystander called as a siren trailed off nearby.

"Thank heaven." Teddy glanced toward the new arrivals, unaware that the *special* agent had suddenly become a pedestrian, or that a tall runner leaving the scene was now a disinterested athlete.

"Okay, move along." Two policemen pushed through the knot of onlookers. One began clearing pedestrians from the street while the other knelt beside the fallen man. A name tag on the kneeling officer's shirt pocket identified him as "Milton."

"We've got paramedics arriving," shouted his buddy.

Officer Milton nodded and got to his feet. "Who saw what happened?" he asked as the cluster of onlookers began leaving the scene.

Paramedics took over CPR efforts, and Teddy brushed at her stiff knees as she stood. She turned to Officer Milton, "He collapsed beside me. I don't know what happened."

"How about you?" Officer Milton turned to the redheaded man strapping on a large backpack.

The youth shook his head. "He suddenly seemed unsteady on his feet. Then…," the redhead waved his hands and shrugged, "he fell."

"Thanks for assisting," Teddy said, gathering her packages.

"Not so fast." Officer Milton ran a hand over his face as if checking his morning's shave. "Let's have your names and your statements. Tell me exactly what you saw." He waited, pencil poised above a notebook. "You first." He nodded at the woman.

"I'm Teddy Sanderson," she said.

"And you?" The officer turned to the youth.

"Connor Douglas."

Teddy, impatient to reach her office, said, "I had just crossed the street when that man bumped me. He took another step or two, and then fell."

"Was a car involved?" The officer stopped writing and looked up.

"No. We were on the sidewalk. I thought he tripped, except he didn't get up."

"I asked if he needed help," interrupted Connor. "He was too far gone to answer. This lady knew CPR, so we started working on him." The youth's brown eyes were bright with excitement.

"And he fell? In that awkward position?" The officer glanced at the fallen man with his legs askew.

Teddy responded, "He got moved slightly when the special agent," she paused and turned to point out the man who had checked the victim's pockets.

"What special agent?" Officer Milton asked.

"I don't see him now." Teddy frowned. "He was here a minute ago." She turned to the young man. "Did you see where he went?"

The redhead shook his head.

"Keep to the point," Officer Milton said. "What special agent?"

"That's who he said he was—a special agent. He was tall, had black hair and a short black beard. He wore sunglasses, and I think English wasn't his first language. He took a badge out of his pocket, but he didn't give me time to read it." Teddy looked at Officer Milton. "He searched the man's pockets for something to explain why he collapsed, but he didn't find anything."

A paramedic approached and handed the officer a credit card. "This is all the I.D. we could find." Behind him the patient was still receiving first aid.

Milton looked at the card. "Does the name Sam Morgan mean anything to either of you?"

Connor looked blank. "Not to me."

Teddy shook her head, but she was frowning. The name seemed familiar. Had she heard it before?

"Officer," the medic continued, "there's a wound on the back of that guy's neck. It's the size of a pin prick, but it's recent and it's been bleeding profusely."

"A fresh wound?" Officer Milton shifted his gaze to Teddy and then to Connor Douglas. He adjusted the radio on his left shoulder and said, "We need crime scene personnel at this location." To Teddy and Connor he said, "We'll need to ask you a few more questions about this *special agent*."

Teddy gave the officer a pleading look. "I have an important appointment. Could I. . . ?"

He shook his head "You're on your way to the station to answer questions. Brody," he called out. "Take these two witnesses to the squad car and keep an eye on them."

Teddy's shoulders slumped. With packages once more in her arms and the tote dangling from one wrist, she gave the officer a last dispirited look. A moment later she and Connor Douglas were escorted to a waiting squad car.

CHAPTER

3

In an irksome turn of events Teddy found herself wedged in an uncomfortable police cruiser beside a lanky young man. Her packages were at their feet. Unable to see into the tote on the floor beside her, she reached in blindly and withdrew her cell phone. She punched in numbers for her friend Frances. "Hi," Teddy greeted when she heard the familiar voice. "I'm going to be late."

"You're never late. What's going on?"

As Teddy explained the situation she heard her friend suck in her breath.

"You've got to be kidding. Where are you? What precinct are they taking you to?"

###

At the word *precinct* Frances's husband of two years, Attorney Gene Ravensworth, drew closer. He noticed his young wife twisting her hair around one finger. It was a habit he'd learned to associate with attacks of heavy-duty stress.

"Want me to take the call?" he whispered in a soothing voice, his hand resting gently on his wife's shoulder.

Nodding, Frances handed her cell phone to him.

"What's going on, Teddy?" he asked, his dark brown eyes resting on his nervous wife. Teddy explained what had happened, ending with the discovery of a wound at the back of the victim's neck. "Where are you now?" Gene asked.

"If you go to a window and look down, you can probably see the flashing lights from the police car I'm sitting in."

Gene moved to the window and looked down. "Okay, I get the picture. As your friend and attorney I'm advising you not to answer any questions until you and I have a chance to talk in private. If this guy was murdered, they may consider you a possible suspect instead of a witness. You said Brody and Milton are the officers at the scene? They're from Central. I'll head there now."

He handed the phone back to Frances. "It looks like our Girl Friday stepped into the middle of a possible homicide." He smiled at his wife and planted a kiss on her worried forehead. "I'll be in touch," he added, hurrying from the room.

"What do you mean you lost the information? Explain." The voice on the phone sounded angry.

Mario tried to reassure the powerful man responsible for directing activities of the Delphi Alliance from somewhere out of the country. Mario explained what had happened, and how Adam had followed the man who somehow intercepted the transfer of information. Yes, Adam had kept the man in sight at all times. No, the man talked to no one. Mario sighed and swiped at perspiration dotting his forehead. Yes, there was no mistake. The fallen man had somehow intercepted and disposed of their important communications.

The excited voice on the phone belonged to a man known to members of Mario's underground cell only as Isaac. None of the cell members had ever met him. However, his wrath was legendary.

"You will be given a matter of days to find what you have lost." The words were spoken slowly, a threat underlying them. "After that," Isaac continued, "members of your family will pay the price of your incompetence. Do you understand me?"

"Yes," Mario whispered. A click in his ear ended their connection. Mario stared into the distance. He and Adam had to find the missing plans. If they didn't, Isaac's threat would be carried out.

"Tell me your name again," Connor said as Teddy punched more numbers on her cell phone.

"I need to make one more quick call," she said, as a voice in her ear responded.

"William Smith Industries, Madge speaking." The voice sounded abrasive.

"This is Teddy Sanderson. I need to speak with Mr. Smith."

"He left early today, Ms. Sanderson. May I take a message?"

"Have him call me as soon as he gets in tomorrow. It's extremely important." Teddy slipped her phone back in her tote. "Sorry to make you wait," she said to Connor. "I'm Teddy Sanderson. Are you a student?"

"Mostly." Connor settled back in the uncomfortable seat.

"Tell me what you saw."

Connor looked at the officer standing near the car and whispered, "I was walking behind you when we crossed the street. I thought you might drop something so I was watching you." He smiled. "I hoped to come to your rescue and then introduce myself."

Teddy returned his smile.

"What I saw," continued Connor, forehead creased in thought, "was this guy bump against you. You turned to look at him and a second or two after that he fell."

Teddy nodded. "I put my packages down so I could check for a pulse. You were checking his breathing passages. Did you notice that bearded man kneeling beside me?"

"Yes, but only briefly. I didn't hear what he said, although I thought he flashed a badge."

"Could you see what it said?"

"He put it away too quickly." Connor took off his thick glasses and began polishing them. "I guess you didn't have time to read it either?"

Teddy shook her head, turning to look out the window. She could see the police and paramedics still at work. "I didn't realize he had gone until I tried to point him out to the officer."

"I wonder why he didn't stick around." Connor slipped the newly polished spectacles back on.

"It looks like he didn't want to get involved," Teddy said.

"But if he's a member of law enforcement…," Conner paused.

"That's assuming he told us the truth or isn't working undercover. His beard and sunglasses will make recognizing him again difficult."

The door to the squad car opened. "No talking," Brody snapped, getting in and adjusting his seat belt. He started the engine.

Teddy and Connor looked at each other, exchanging smiles as the car moved forward. Officer Brody was too late with his command to keep silent.

"Are you taking us to Central?" Teddy asked.

"Yes," Brody responded.

"My attorney is there. I'm not to answer questions until I've had a chance to talk to him."

"Damned attorneys," Brody mumbled. "Always telling witnesses to *lawyer up*."

"Really?" Connor whispered. "Should I refuse to answer questions, too?"

Teddy leaned toward him. "My attorney said that if the dead man was murdered, we could become suspects."

"I said, *no talking*," Brody growled from the front seat.

"*Thanks*." Connor mouthed the word while scribbling his name and phone number on a piece of notepaper. He passed the information to Teddy.

The action made her smile. It was like being in school and passing notes behind the teacher's back. She tucked Connor's information into her coat pocket and reached into her tote. It took only a minute to pull out the box of business cards. She opened it and handed a card to Connor, then smiled at the startled look on his face.

"What's a Girl Friday," he whispered.

"It's a woman with a wide range of abilities and duties. Sometimes we're referred to as paralegals." Teddy smiled. "I do work for a group of attorneys. They're my clients."

"I said *no talking*," Brody yelled.

With a frown, parole officer Gwen Morgan studied the file of the new parolee who would soon join her in her office at the Law Enforcement Building. She dreaded the session that lay ahead. Myron Ratini had been sentenced to a ten-year term in state prison on a manslaughter charge concerning the death of a retired handyman. With time off for good behavior, Ratini had served only four years and a few months.

"And now I get him," Gwen muttered, wondering if rehab had changed him at all. To fortify herself, she smoothed her graying hair, refreshed her lipstick, and pulled out the checklist she would discuss with her new client. If he broke any of the conditions, he would find himself back in prison, serving the remainder of his sentence. She noted one condition was to avoid contact with his former wife, a woman he had at one time been charged with trying to murder. Gwen had searched unsuccessfully for the former Mrs. Ratini. She needed to be warned of her ex-husband's release.

As Gwen pondered what she would say to her new parolee, two floors below, the former Teddy Sanderson Ratini was in conversation with her attorney.

"My advice, Teddy," said Gene Ravensworth unbuttoning his tweed jacket, "is for you to give honest answers, but be brief. Do not go into detail. And do not explain what it is you meant by answering as you did."

"I can do that," Teddy assured him. "Just get me out of here." The room they sat in seemed drab, perhaps even hostile with its gray paint and lack of windows.

Gene understood Teddy's eagerness to leave. He knew she was preparing to start a new business in a room across the hall from his own offices. "Now then," he said, "let me ask you a couple of questions. Did you know the dead man or had you ever seen him before?"

"Not to my knowledge."

"That's not the same as yes or no. Is that because you think you might have seen him before?"

"It's because," she lowered her voice and leaned close. "For a minute, just before he died, he looked right at me. It was as if he recognized me. I bent down and it almost sounded like he spoke." She stared at her friend.

"What do you mean?"

"His lips didn't move so I couldn't be sure, but for an instant I thought he whispered my name." She shuddered at the memory.

"Anything else?"

She nodded. "I think he tried to say something else, or repeat what he'd already said, but I'm not sure. It almost sounded like he'd breathed out the word *take* but maybe he was trying to say my name again."

The door opened suddenly and Officer Milton marched into the room. He slammed the door behind him and glared at Teddy. "Okay, Ms. Sanderson, when was the last time before today that you saw Sam Morgan?" He towered over Teddy, his feet spread and his arms crossed over his thick chest.

"Sam Morgan?" It was Gene who asked the question. "Is that the victim's name?"

"We can get to your questions later, councilor." Officer Milton frowned at the interruption. "Right now I'm asking the questions and I want your client's answers."

"I'll need time alone with my client before she answers," Gene said. He had turned pale and his voice cracked.

"You've had time together. Now, it's my turn." Officer Milton moved closer to underscore his point.

"Read my lips, Milton," Gene said. "Either we get a few more minutes alone or I advise my client not to answer."

"Okay, okay." Officer Milton backed away, a sarcastic expression playing across his face as he turned to leave.

"And turn off the speaker system," Gene called to the officer's departing back. He moved close to Teddy, putting his lips next to her ear. "You *do* know Sam Morgan, Teddy. Don't speak when you recall why you know him. Just nod."

Teddy shook her head to indicate the name still wasn't familiar to her.

Gene whispered, "Two years ago, at my wedding, he was the best man."

Teddy pulled away to stare at her friend.

Gene leaned forward, "The wedding where you were maid of honor and walked down the aisle after the ceremony with my best man and best friend," he paused, "Sam Morgan of the Federal Bureau of Investigation."

Teddy clasped her hands to her face; her eyes wide. She nodded. Of course! She remembered now. She'd met Gene's best man only moments before the wedding ceremony because he'd missed the rehearsal dinner and couldn't stay for the reception. But the handsome man in a tuxedo couldn't possibly be the same Sam Morgan she'd seen dying on a public sidewalk.

"Don't worry," Gene whispered, grief twisting his features. "This scene is about to shift from Central Precinct to the FBI offices in the Stettler Building—on the floor above your office and mine."

CHAPTER

4

The telephone rang in the office of the *News Telegrapher's* legal counsel. "What's troubling you, Maxwell?"

"I have a question dealing with potential liability," said the newspaper's editor. "We want to run a story speculating on FBI matters as they impact a member of the public. If I brought you a copy of a story we're thinking about running, could you let me know how close to the edge of a lawsuit we'd be skating?"

"Bring it over and I'll give you my best advice."

The editor turned to his reporter. "You'll know the outcome of my meeting if your story shows up on page one tomorrow. That will mean you can go ahead with your plans. Just be sure you always meet the deadline."

"I'm on it." The crime reporter did a little dance after leaving the editor's office. Meeting deadlines was a reporter's way of life.

###

How do reporters get details that officials want to keep secret? Teddy Sanderson tossed the morning newspaper into the wastebasket and reached for her cold coffee. She drained the cup in one gulp.

The *News Telegrapher's* account of Sam Morgan's death stated that FBI investigators were examining images caught by surveillance cameras near the scene of Sam's death. They expected to reveal a person of interest soon.

Unfortunately, the story also revealed Teddy's name and her office location on the floor below the FBI's Resident Agency where the dead man had been employed. Whatever news source the reporter used omitted only one detail—Connor Douglas wasn't mentioned by name. He was referred to only as a bystander who assisted Teddy with CPR.

Teddy slammed her empty cup on her desk. Even the disappearing agent was mentioned in greater detail than the helpful young man.

Curbing her desire to call the newspaper and complain, she looked around her new office. Because her friend Frances had done a fine job of organizing things, Teddy was ready to start work on assignments she'd received from the attorneys across the hall at Booker and Ravensworth. She pushed the packages of office supplies purchased the day before into a cupboard behind her desk. Once she finished with today's FBI session, she'd have time to unwrap things.

Today Special Agent Dillard Brighton wanted to go over details of her story as reported yesterday, and he wanted more details. Her story had been repeated so many times, she'd finally written it down. What more could she tell anyone about the man who died beside her?

It was time she got in touch with William Smith. She needed to tell him what she'd discovered about his wife's current activities. Teddy picked up the telephone and dialed his number just as a brief knock sounded on her office door. Gene Ravensworth poked his head into the room, and Teddy waved at him. "Just a minute," she mouthed, as her call was being answered.

"William Smith Industries, Madge speaking."

"This is Teddy Sanderson. I need to speak with Mr. Smith."

"He's late this morning, Ms. Sanderson. May I take a message?"

"Have him call me as soon as he arrives. It's extremely important." Teddy looked at Gene as she hung up. His eyes had dark circles under them.

"I understand we're to wait here," he said. "They'll pick us up and escort us to the fifth floor. Have you thought of any more details concerning Sam's death?"

Teddy shook her head. "I tried, but I couldn't think of a thing. You look like you didn't sleep any better than I did last night." She tried to keep her voice light. The loss of a best friend had to be devastating.

"Sam was special to me," Gene said. "We'd been friends since law school."

"We tried to save him, Gene."

"I know." He gave her a sad smile and cleared his throat. "Something must have gone wrong with his assignment. I'm assuming, of course, that his death is related to FBI matters."

Behind Gene the door opened. "Waiting for an escort?" Agent Brighton's secretary smiled as she entered.

Gene straightened his shoulders and nodded.

Teddy shoved her tote under her desk and pushed the new swivel chair in front of it. Grabbing her keys, she followed Gene and Helen Grisham, pausing only to lock the office door. "Can't we take the stairs?" She pointed to the staircase beside her office.

Helen shook her head. "There isn't any way to enter a secure floor from the stairwell side."

Teddy looked startled. "No doors, huh? I can see that having an office in the Stettler is going to be an interesting experience."

Today, instead of running clothes, Adam Bailey wore a well-tailored black suit. He cut a striking figure as he headed toward the Stettler Building, a leather briefcase tucked under one arm. The briefcase was almost empty, but it gave the impression he was a successful businessman.

He glanced at his watch. Ten thirty. Perfect. Finding the woman who tried to help the FBI agent was easy, thanks to the newspaper. If she wasn't in her office this morning, he could search it and leave, but if she was there, her fate would be the same as the FBI agent's.

Adam's face hardened. He pushed through the Stettler's large glass doors, pausing briefly to take a deep breath. He continued across the lobby to the elevators, his heart pounding. *What if the FBI has my picture? What if they have surveillance cameras trained on me?* He tried not to search for cameras as he crossed the lobby. *Am I walking into a trap?*

Beads of sweat glistened on his forehead. He pulled a handkerchief from his pocket, but resisted the urge to wipe his face with it. He must not draw attention to himself. The lives of family members depended on that.

It was this morning's conversation with Mario that made him nervous. "If you don't get this right. . . ." Mario's voice had trailed off, but his meaning was clear. "We can have no more *screw-ups*. Isaac has granted us a few days to fix things. After that our families will be in danger."

Adam shuddered. Why should Mario, a long-time friend, blame him for the lost information? It had been gone before he reached the drop site. Mario had left too soon. *He* was the one at fault.

The elevator doors opened and Adam stepped in. Two young men entered beside him, but neither spoke. They both left at the second floor. On the third floor Adam stepped from the elevator, and moved quickly to the stairs. He opened the door and walked up one flight. At the fourth floor, he paused to gulp a deep breath; then he stepped into the hallway.

To his right was the elevator and beyond it, the public restrooms. On the other side of the hall, at the far end, was a second stairwell. Offices lined both sides of the hall with numbered doors and plaques with company names. When Adam passed the men's room, a heavy-set, curly-haired man exited. Adam nodded, but the man ignored him and walked in the opposite direction.

Myron Ratini put his comb away as he headed toward the nearest stairwell. A moment later he paused beside office number 454—*Bishop's Music School*. A very nervous man had just passed him and was heading down the hall. The man's demeanor, familiar to Myron after four years in prison, piqued his curiosity.

At the far end of the hall, the man stopped beside the office door with a plaque reading: *T. Sanderson, Girl Friday*. Myron had checked that door himself and knew it was locked. The nervous man tried to enter, but found he couldn't. When he didn't leave, Myron returned to the men's room and began watching through the doorway he left ajar.

The stranger twisted the doorknob again before glancing down the deserted hall. Following that, he reached into his briefcase and removed something he used to fiddle with the lock. Suddenly the door opened and the stranger stepped inside, closing the door behind him.

"Fancy that," Myron whispered, a smirk spreading across his face. The idea that someone else wanted to create trouble for his ex-wife was an intriguing development. Perhaps this stranger could be persuaded to do the thing that had consumed Myron's thoughts every day of the four years he'd spent in prison. Maybe the man who had just broken into Teddy's office could be persuaded to kill her.

Inside the vacant office, Adam surveyed his surroundings. His plan called for a quick, but thorough search with no mistakes. He turned back to the door, twisted the dead bolt and pushed in the button on the handle. Two locks would buy him time if the woman returned before he finished.

Yesterday she'd carried packages and a handbag. Had the Alliance's information found its way into her things? Adam looked at the table behind the woman's desk where a cupboard door, partially open, revealed a stack of packages. Three steps and Adam stood beside the cabinet, reaching for the first package. He tore wrappings from it, revealing only copy paper. He pushed the package back in the cupboard and reached for a second parcel. Again no Alliance plans. Within minutes everything was unwrapped. Books, paper, pens and file folders were back in the cupboard, but no Alliance plans. His search left wrappings on the floor behind the woman's desk. Those, he kicked out of sight before turning to check the desk's drawers. All were empty.

Adam noticed a small box sitting off to one side. It contained business cards. He took one and closed the lid. His heart racing, he again surveyed the room. Where was the lady's handbag? Did she have it with her? He checked file cabinet drawers and found nothing. He moved to the wastebasket—a discarded newspaper; nothing more.

At the space behind the desk where the woman would sit, was her chair. Adam pulled it away from the desk, suddenly aware of a voice in the hall and a shadow on the office door's frosted glass window.

Adam tensed. He thought of the small poisoned dart in his briefcase and waited, breathing hard. With any luck the visitor would leave after discovering the door was locked.

"It's like déjà vu," a woman said. "Whoever has been in this hallway recently is wearing the same strong aftershave my ex-husband wore. It makes me shiver. Thank goodness Myron's still locked up."

"Calm down, Teddy." It was a man's voice. "You look like you've seen a ghost."

"Just the smell of that aftershave and I'm a nervous wreck. I'm sorry to be slow, Gene. My keys are here somewhere."

"Take your time."

Not visitors who would go away! Someone with keys! Adam whirled, eyes wide. Where could he hide? A key was already unlocking the deadbolt. *Fool,* he thought, blood pulsing in his ears. *You didn't plan an escape!*

His eyes darted to the file cabinet and the door beside it. He grabbed his briefcase, and stepped through the doorway into what appeared to be a workroom. A table and a few chairs sat near a copy machine. Beyond the copier was another door. Did it lead to a bathroom or a closet where he would be trapped? Poised beside the second door, he waited, breathing hard. He heard the hall door in the next room open.

"I could have sworn I only locked the deadbolt," the woman said.

"We all do things out of habit," the man answered. "Especially in times of stress, and you're under a lot of stress right now."

"Give me a minute and I'll make a copy for you," the woman responded.

A chill traveled Adam's body. In panic he tried the door next to him. Miraculously it opened to the hallway! He wasn't trapped! The woman's workroom had its own entrance. As quietly as he could, Adam stepped into the hall, pulling the door shut behind him. Taking long strides, he put as much distance as he could between himself and the woman's office. His whole body trembled.

As he approached the elevator, its doors opened. He stepped inside.

"Excuse me," said a redheaded man with glasses as he left the elevator, a baseball cap in his hands.

Adam glanced at the man. *I have seen this man before; but where?*

"Hold the elevator!" The voice came from the left—out of Adam's line of sight.

The young man's arm shot out to break the elevator door's sensor.

Hobbling toward the elevator was a man on crutches too short for his tall body. One hand gripped a violin case. At that moment, a man stepped from the men's room and hurried to the crippled man's side.

Adam cringed. He didn't want to wait. He wanted out of this building before FBI agents captured him.

"Thanks for waiting," the man with crutches said, stepping into the elevator. He turned to the man beside him. "And thank you for carrying my violin. I can take it now."

"No trouble," Myron replied as the violin case changed hands. "I was heading this way myself."

As the elevator doors began closing, the man who left the elevator glanced back. Framed in the space between the closing doors was an anxious-looking face that nagged him. He couldn't recall where he'd seen it recently, but he'd remember shortly. Memories always surfaced eventually.

"My partner and I were glad to help you find this space," Gene said, stuffing the paper Teddy copied for him in his briefcase. "Once you get settled and hire some help, your second room will come in handy." He looked around the office. Teddy was a computer expert—fast and accurate. As a Girl Friday with paralegal experience, she knew her way around the courthouse and various businesses in town. She was a good editor and was skilled at interviewing witnesses. Having her across the hall from Booker and Ravensworth Attorneys was a real advantage.

"Could I offer you some coffee?" Teddy asked.

"No thanks. I need to get back to the office and prepare for tomorrow's trial."

Teddy studied Gene's face. "What I don't understand," she said, "is what Agent Brighton meant when he said the intercept Sam hoped to make may have taken place. Is that why he was killed? If Sam intercepted something that belonged to the Delphi Alliance, where is it now? Did the people he took it from get it back when they killed him? And if the FBI doesn't know where the drop was to be made, how did Sam know? It doesn't make sense he'd keep that kind of information to himself."

"You ask a lot of questions and I don't know any of the answers," Gene responded. The weary look was back on his face. "Everyone may be waiting to see if there's an attempt by the Delphi Alliance to recover whatever Sam may have intercepted. If there is, the FBI will know for sure Sam got away with something important. The question then will be, what did he do with it?"

"How will the FBI know if an attempt is made?"

"Add that to your list of questions I can't answer." They walked from the workroom into Teddy's office. "I need to get back to work and you need to finish preparing the jury instructions and trial memorandum for tomorrow's trial." Gene moved toward the door.

"I'll get started on that right after I put away the supplies I bought yesterday." Teddy gestured behind her, realizing for the first time that the cupboard door was ajar. She gasped. The packages she purchased yesterday were unwrapped. Moving in that direction, she saw paper and plastic bags on the floor behind her desk.

"What's the matter?" Gene had turned back.

"My packages were still wrapped when we left for Brighton's office!" Teddy's eyes were wide. "They aren't now."

Gene moved to her side. "You've had a visitor. Has anything else been disturbed?"

Teddy looked around, noting details. "My tote is still under the desk but my chair isn't as I left it. There wasn't anything for a thief to steal, except office supplies and the tote."

"How about money?"

"I had my wallet with me in case I needed I.D." She patted her jacket pocket.

"This may be what the FBI is waiting for," Gene said. "We'll ask Brighton." He began punching numbers on his cell phone.

###

The elevator containing Adam, Myron Ratini and the music student on crutches reached the lobby. Adam pushed past the others and was soon out of the building.

Looking calm and composed, but walking just as fast was Teddy's ex-husband.

In the parking lot behind the Stettler Building Adam got into a dark green sedan. A short distance away Myron hopped into a black Accord. The vehicles left the lot, one after the other, headed in the same direction.

When Adam drove into a busy neighborhood where a seedy little cafe known as the Corner Coffeehouse was located, he maneuvered his sedan into a tight parking slot a few doors away. A moment later he rushed back to the coffeehouse.

Isaac insisted cell members avoid meeting one another, but Adam and Mario had been friends before becoming members of the Delphi Alliance. Sometimes they just seemed to need coffee at the same time, served at the same place.

Myron circled the block and finally found a parking space where he could observe the green sedan he'd been following. He sat back and waited. When the nervous man left the coffeehouse, Myron would follow. If the coffeehouse was a favorite stop for the burglar, then Myron would frequent it with a listening device so sensitive it could pick up whispered conversations from across the room. He'd learned about things like that during his years in prison. Very soon now, he'd know what the break-in at Teddy's office was all about. He smiled and waited. He'd spent his four years in prison planning her demise, but he didn't have a deadline A few more hours wouldn't make a huge difference.

While Gene talked to Agent Brighton, Teddy opened the file in which she had reports concerning the coming divorce of William and Sally Anne Smith. She punched in William's office number on her cell phone. He needed to know about the life insurance policies Sally Anne had taken out on him. Especially, he needed to know about the double indemnity clauses.

A familiar raspy voice came on the line. "William Smith Industries, Madge speaking."

"This is Teddy Sanderson again. Is Mr. Smith available now?"

"Ms. Sanderson, I was about to call you. Mr. Smith was taken to Sacred Heart Hospital an hour ago. He was in a traffic accident this morning."

Teddy closed her eyes. She could feel her heart racing. "Are his injuries serious?" She thought of the man old enough to be her grandfather.

"He has a few broken bones; but nothing life-threatening. Some guy ran a stop sign and broadsided him."

Teddy lowered her voice, "Was it a hit-and-run?"

Madge gasped. "How did you know?"

CHAPTER
5

As Teddy hung up the phone, the door behind Gene opened. "Are you open for business?" A redheaded young man walked in.

"Connor," Teddy greeted. "Come in."

The lanky youth nodded. "Agent Brighton told me to wait here for an escort."

Teddy extended her hand in greeting. "Gene, this is Connor Douglas, the man who helped do CPR on Sam. Connor, meet Gene Ravensworth, my friend and my client."

Gene put his cell phone in his briefcase and reached out to shake hands. "Sam Morgan was my best friend. Thank you for trying to save him."

"Of course."

Gene turned to Teddy. "Agent Brighton said we're not to touch anything. He's sending someone to check for fingerprints."

Connor looked at Teddy. "Fingerprints? What's going on?" He looked confused. When she didn't answer, he turned to Gene, "Does anyone know why Mr. Morgan was murdered?"

"I don't think so," Gene replied.

"Perhaps you should ask the *News Telegrapher's* crime reporter," Teddy said. "He seems to have all the answers."

Connor said, "I saw that story. What a lot of details."

Teddy met his eyes. "That's just it. There were too many details. Except for your involvement, that reporter seemed to know everything."

Gene said, "I wonder why he didn't include you in the story?"

Connor ran fingers through his hair. "The article mentioned a man offering assistance. I took that to mean me."

"Mentioning an anonymous individual isn't the same as all my personal details that got reported," Teddy complained.

There was an awkward silence. "It didn't occur to me I'd been left out."

"I wish the article hadn't been so detailed." Teddy reached out to close a desk drawer, but checked her impulse.

Connor watched her restless movements. "Maybe the article will bring you some new clients."

"What it may have brought me is a burglar."

"What do you mean?"

"I mean someone broke into this office while Gene and I were with the FBI this morning. They unwrapped the purchases I made yesterday."

Connor's gaze shifted between Teddy and Gene. "And you think that's connected with Sam's death? Why would his murderers care what you bought?"

Gene shrugged his shoulders and ignored Connor's questions. "Teddy, Agent Brighton wants you to check with the other offices on this floor. See if they've had break-ins." He closed his briefcase. "I'll ask my partner if we've had anything unusual happen on our side of the hall this morning."

"I'll talk to the others," Teddy said, "but afterward I'm going to the *News Telegrapher* and have a word or two with their crime reporter. I may be able to sue him for invasion of privacy or something."

Gene laughed. "Unless it was slander, I doubt you'd have a case."

"If I wouldn't be intruding, I'd like to help," Connor offered. "You check your neighbors and as soon as I'm finished with the FBI this morning, I'll head for the newspaper office and talk to their crime reporter."

Gene headed for the door. "I'll leave you two to work things out, but I need those trial papers before noon, Teddy." He opened the door. "Nice meeting you, Connor, and again, thanks for trying to help my buddy."

"Nice guy," Connor said, as the door closed behind Gene. "Do you want to suggest what I should say to Bradford?"

Teddy thought for a minute. "He invaded my privacy by revealing too much personal information. I thought newspapers left things like that vague. You know, *woman in the Stettler Building,* or *pedestrian on the sidewalk.* Not *Teddy Sanderson on the fourth floor, office number four hundred.* The only thing omitted was that this office is at the end of the hall where there's a burned out light bulb."

Connor laughed. "If your break-in was related to Morgan's death, then it may mean he had something that someone else wants. Something he stashed before he died."

"And the murderer thought it got mixed up with my packages?" Teddy glanced at the messy floor behind her desk.

"That's exciting to think about. I wonder what kind of case Sam was working on?"

Teddy checked her watch. "Where's that fingerprint expert?" She got to her feet. "I have work to do."

Connor seemed deep in thought. "Whatever Sam was involved in was important enough for someone to kill him." His eyes locked with Teddy's. The image of the FBI agent's death hung in the air between them. "If he got hold of something, what could he have done with it?"

Teddy's eyes narrowed. "How the heck should I know? You're not suggesting he slipped me something, are you? If he had, would I be holding out on the FBI? Do you think I'm stupid?"

"Of course not." Connor blushed. "That's not what I meant."

The phone rang and Teddy reached for it with a tissue.

"Girl Friday, Sanderson speaking!" She listened. "I'll tell him." Teddy hung up the receiver and turned to Connor. "They're ready for you upstairs. They'll meet you at the elevators."

Connor took a step toward the door. "I'll call you after I've talked to Bradford."

"Tell him to lay off."

Connor nodded and opened the door. A man in a business suit was just preparing to enter.

"Ms. Sanderson?" the stranger said, moving past Connor. He had a badge in one hand and a small case in the other. "I'm Special Agent

Jackson. I'll make as little mess as possible, and I should be finished by the time you've talked to your neighbors."

###

Teddy stopped at the first door she came to. The sign beside it read "Taylor Maid." She gave the door a couple of polite raps, then opened it and walked in.

"Hello," she said, greeting the bent figure of a gray-haired woman attaching a paper pattern to a piece of white satin spread across a long table.

"May I help you?" the woman asked.

"I'm your new neighbor, Teddy Sanderson—in the office next door."

The seamstress smiled. "I'm delighted to meet you. I'm Alice Taylor, the *maid* who specializes in wedding gowns. Won't you have a seat?" She gestured toward a chair. "It's been lonely at this end of the hall. Maybe management will replace the burned out light bulb now that you've moved in."

Teddy studied the older woman. "Do you know if anyone on this floor is having problems with burglaries?"

"Goodness," Alice exclaimed. "I can't think why anyone would break into offices on this floor. None of us keeps much cash around. There's an investment broker on the other side of me; then an insurance company. Bishop's Music School has the last two spaces with Booker and Ravensworth Attorneys on the other side of the hall."

"It doesn't sound like there should be much traffic to this floor."

"Bishops have students arriving several times a day, but my clients only come once or twice a week. I don't know how often the others see people, although the attorneys have clients showing up regularly. Have you had a problem?"

"Yes," Teddy said.

"Oh my," Alice responded. "You should notify the building superintendent."

"That's a good idea," Teddy said, waving as she opened the door and started down the hall. It didn't take long to learn that no one else on the fourth floor had recently been burglarized.

###

"Have you talked to your neighbors?" Connor asked when he phoned that afternoon. "Were other offices entered?"

"No. What happened when you talked to Bradford?"

Connor replied, "He was chasing down another story. No one knew when to expect him back. I considered speaking to his editor, but he was in a board meeting. I'll keep trying to see Bradford since you're busy getting papers ready for a trial."

"Tell him to check his health insurance policy. He's going to need good coverage when I get finished with him."

CHAPTER

6

The above-the-fold, page-one story in the *News Telegrapher* the next morning began, "Law enforcement officials tight-lipped." It went on to explain that developments in the search for the killer of FBI agent Sam Morgan were confidential. The story said that surveillance footage from stores near the crime scene would be studied. The article by C. Bradford hinted that the FBI was also evaluating Sam's murder as it might relate to a recent break-in at Teddy Sanderson's office. The story ended with: *An unofficial source suggests that if Sam Morgan intercepted something that his murderers want back and it wasn't found on his person, one of those close to him as he died may have ended up with it.*

Teddy's office door burst open. "Teddy!" Frances Ravensworth rushed into the room, a copy of the *News Telegrapher* clutched in her hand. "Have you seen the headlines? This story makes it sound like you have whatever Sam intercepted. That could put your life in danger." She slapped the newspaper on her friend's desk.

"Calm down, Frances," Teddy said, getting to her feet. "I don't have whatever it is everyone is looking for." She headed for the coffee pot.

Frances sat down, but scooted forward, resting her elbows on Teddy's desk. "Well you know it and now I know it, but that crime reporter doesn't. You should set up shop somewhere else until this thing blows over."

"I won't do that," Teddy replied, her voice firm and calm as she poured coffee for her friend.

Frances's hands trembled when she reached for the coffee. "I'm worried about you." She took a sip.

Teddy returned to her seat behind the desk. "I spent most of yesterday sending out notices telling people where they could find me. I'm not going into hiding."

"We know you're a great cook." Frances nodded at the coffee cup she held, and drained it. "Why don't you open a bistro somewhere?"

Teddy's phone rang. "I've got to take this call, Frances. I need clients. I'll see you later. Stop worrying." Teddy picked up the receiver, "Girl Friday, Sanderson speaking." She waved as Frances left the office.

"Teddy?" The excited voice on the phone was Connor's. "Did you see the morning paper?"

"Of course I did. What a lot of innuendo and half-truths. The idea that you or I might have whatever it was Sam stole from the Delphi Alliance is ridiculous. How can that reporter speculate on such things? Either you get him stopped or I'm calling his editor."

"I'll confront them," Connor said. "Today for sure."

"As soon as I tie down a couple of things I'm going to make Bradford and his editor wish they'd concentrated on printing the comics."

"You won't need to do that; I'm en route to the *News Telegrapher* right now. I'll call you as soon as I have it out with Bradford."

"Tell him to stick to fairy tales. He obviously doesn't understand the difference between fact and fiction."

Teddy delivered papers to the courthouse for her clients, then abruptly made a decision. *She* was the one who needed to confront the *News Telegrapher*'s psychic reporter, not Connor. She'd been stewing about the newspaper's story ever since Frances burst into her office, and Connor's phone call hadn't helped. *She* was the one who needed to make the reporter understand the problems his articles created for her.

Within minutes Teddy was marching up to the *News Telegrapher*'s reception desk, asking to see a crime reporter named Bradford.

"Down the hall and to your left," the receptionist said, pointing toward an open area where more than a dozen people worked at computers. "You can't miss him. Bradford is the guy at the back of the room."

"Thanks," Teddy said, heading for the newsroom's farthest workstation.

At that moment a paper airplane soared through the air, barely missing the heads of several newsroom occupants. Laughing at the success of the flight was a lanky youth with thick lenses. Teddy stopped mid-step.

Connor Douglas choked back his laughter and leaped from the desk where he'd been sitting. He retrieved the plane and handed it to another individual who prepared it for flight. Was the man now holding the plane Bradford?

Teddy whirled, returning to the reception desk. "Does Mr. Bradford already have someone with him?" If Connor had been successful setting up a person-to-person meeting with the reporter, interrupting them might not be to her advantage.

"I think he's alone." The receptionist leaned back in her chair to view the staff in the newsroom. "Yep, he's alone. His desk is clear at the back. Connor Bradford Douglas." She turned to her ringing phone. "*News Telegrapher.* May I help you?"

Teddy stared at the young man happily sailing paper airplanes. For a minute she couldn't move. "I j–just realized I have another appointment," she said to the busy receptionist. "I'll see Mr. Bradford later."

Teddy headed for her car, fists curled, arms swinging at her sides.

Couldn't get in to see him, he said. She increased her pace until she was running. *He'll try again.* She fought angry tears. "Damn you, Connor," she shouted. "Try looking in a mirror if you want to see that reporter."

Reaching her red Corolla, she bumped the alarm button before jamming the right key into the door lock. Bumping the alarm button set off the car's alarm. A lot of tooting and beeping followed. She jumped back, depressing the alarm button several times before the noise stopped. Unlocking the car door, she flung herself into the driver's seat.

Why is Connor doing this to me? Is my CPR buddy counting on me leaving the interview with Bradford up to him? No wonder there wasn't any mention of Connor by name in the newspaper. She jammed her foot against the gas pedal and pumped wildly, an action that flooded the engine. When the motor wouldn't start, her temper flared. "Damn, damn, damn."

Her face burned. She had trusted Connor and he'd lied to her. She'd trusted her ex-husband too and not only had he lied; he'd tried to kill her.

Well, things were changing. Myron was serving a much deserved jail term, and the traitorous Connor Bradford Douglas would soon be the recipient of some well-deserved revenge.

Teddy reached for her tote and plunged her hand deep inside looking for a breath mint. "Now what?" she asked, pulling an unfamiliar CD out. She didn't remember putting it in her tote. Was it like the deadbolt on her office door that she hadn't remembered locking? Had she put a CD from her music collection into her tote and then forgotten about it?

Teddy read the label, *The Sound of Music*. It looked like her recording. She shrugged her shoulders. The stress of the last twenty-four hours was draining her.

And then she smiled. Frances probably slipped the music into her tote during her visit this morning, hoping to cheer Teddy up. She'd done things like that in the past. Having decided that riddle was solved, Teddy put the CD back in her tote and waited for her flooded engine to start.

"I'm here to see William Smith." Teddy waited while the sixth floor nurse responded by pointing to room 629.

"Teddy," Bill Smith greeted as she walked into his private room. "I was hoping my secretary could reach you. Thanks for all the reports you sent over. Sally Anne's attorney was at the hospital harassing me even before the doctor set my leg. You can't guess what it is Sally Anne wants." Bill was the CEO and chairman of the Board of Directors of the largest privately held electric plant in the state—Peoples Power Plant.

"I bet Sally Anne wants all you have. Does that include your interest in Peoples Power?"

"Not unless it's destroyed. Then she'd like the cash."

Teddy pulled a chair to the side of his bed. "I've discovered something else that should interest you." She noticed deep lines and vivid bruising etched around William's eyes.

"I'm listening." He shut his eyes tightly before opening them. "Let me have it."

"She's taken out life insurance policies on you—several of them; all with double indemnity clauses. She's the beneficiary." Teddy watched the injured man's startled response.

His eyelids fluttered, and then opened wide. "That's twice the money if I die in an accident. Are you suggesting yesterday's hit-and-run was a deliberate attempt on my life?"

"I think you have to consider that as a possibility. When the police find the other driver, they'll certainly have some questions for him."

"My insurance company dug up a couple of witnesses. They said the truck that hit me had a unique bumper on the front, something they called a bull-bar winch-bumper."

"Did they get the license number of the truck, or see how many occupants were in it?"

"It was a dark blue vehicle without plates, and it had only one occupant. My insurance agent said that a truck with a bull-bar winch would most likely belong to an off-road enthusiast, a logger, or someone doing recovery work. The police said if that heavy winch had hit on the driver's side of my car, I'd be dead."

"A truck with special equipment? That should make it easy to find."

"Unless the winch was only bolted on instead of welded in place."

"Would it be all right with you if I keep nosing around?"

"Go ahead, but if Sally Anne is involved, then you should check out Hill Huggers."

"What's that?"

"It's an off-road recreation group. Sally Anne belonged to it for a while."

"Local?"

"Yes."

"I'll see what I can find out. How long will you be in the hospital?"

"A day. Maybe two. I'll head home as soon as I can manage on my own—with the aid of a private nurse, of course."

Teddy smiled. "I'll see what I can dig up. In the meantime, make sure your private nurse isn't a friend of Sally Anne's."

###

"You were lucky I had a cancellation," Sally Anne Smith said, as she scrubbed her new customer's hair.

"I was contemplating a murder when I saw your sign." Teddy had introduced herself as Ella Jones. "Having my hair done is a good alternative. You are saving the jerk's life by working me in." She smiled, alert to how her mention of a murder registered with the petite, auburn-haired woman.

Sally Anne rinsed Teddy's soapy hair, added a conditioner, and after a few minutes rinsed it out. She patted the hair with a towel as they walked to her station. "Man troubles?"

"Do women have any other kind?" Teddy asked, settling comfortably in Sally Anne's chair.

"A husband?" Sally Anne smeared a little gel between her palms and rubbed it into the blond curls.

"No, thank goodness. Someone I trusted lied to me."

Sally Anne trimmed a few hairs. "But not someone you really plan to do away with?"

Teddy whispered, "I'm still making up my mind on that. If you know of any alligator-infested ponds or someone to help create one. . . ." She smiled, not completing the thought. The picture of Connor swimming frantically among alligators fit her mood perfectly.

Sally Anne laughed. "I don't personally know of any such ponds, but I might know some guys who won't object to crocodile capers."

"Maybe I'll organize a list of deserving people and contact your friends," Teddy said. With a sigh she leaned back in the chair and listened to various conversations around her. She was hoping she had enough cash to pay for the impulsive appointment. When using the name Ella Jones, it wouldn't do to write checks or use credit cards with the name Teddy Sanderson on them.

CHAPTER

7

With an admiring glance at her hair, Teddy paid Sally Anne in cash and left the shop. Unfortunately, she kept thinking of Connor. What if his column gave someone ideas about information she didn't have? They'd come after her. Didn't he realize the danger he put her in? And if he actually *did* realize the danger, was her safety less important than possible awards for his front-page stories?

Hoping to relax as she drove, Teddy punched the play button for the CD she'd found in her tote. She sighed as the beginning notes from *The Sound of Music* drifted around her. Before the first song ended, she felt more relaxed, and thanks to the parking transponder in her car, she parked in the Stettler's secure garage without pausing to identify herself.

At her office, before entering, she made sure the door's locks were as she'd left them. The blinking telephone signaled missed calls and she hurriedly made notes of the callers. When a message from a woman named Gwen Morgan played, Teddy immediately called her back.

"Mrs. Morgan, this is Teddy Sanderson returning your call. I want you to know how sorry I am about Sam's death."

"I know. Thank you for trying to help him. There wasn't anything you or anyone else could have done." There was a pause. "I'm a parole officer, Ms. Sanderson. I'm tidying up loose ends before I take some time off. Because you assumed your maiden name after your divorce,

I've had difficulty finding you. Therefore, I'm two days late notifying you that your ex-husband has been paroled."

Teddy sucked in a deep breath. "Myron's out? He can't be. He was sentenced to ten years."

Gwen continued. "He was released the day before yesterday, on good behavior."

"Good Lord." Teddy reached for the arm of her chair to steady herself.

"He has several conditions to his release, and one of them involves you. He is not to go within fifty yards of you, and he's not to communicate with you in any way."

"And if he does?" Teddy's throat tightened, remembering the scent of Myron's aftershave in the hall outside her office door.

"If he doesn't abide by the terms of his parole, then we want to know. If you have proof and it's sufficient, we'll drop him behind bars for the remainder of his sentence."

Mario and Adam faced each other across a small table in the Corner Coffeehouse. Mario brushed cigarette ashes off the table as he lectured his friend. "I've told you many times. Plan your escape before all else. Haven't I always said that?" He tested the temperature of his coffee, frowning at Adam over the rim of the cup as he drank.

Adam stared into the thick Turkish drink in front of him. "Yes," he mumbled. "You always have said that, but I was hurrying. I wanted to look through things before the woman returned." He met his friend's gaze before nervously glancing around the room. Men in work clothes sat smoking, staring into coffee cups as they carried on whispered conversations. One occupant sat alone, a newspaper close to his face, and an empty coffee cup beside him. He had ear phones in both ears.

Behind the newspaper, Myron turned up the volume on the special listening device installed in what looked like a pack of cigarettes.

The fake pack was in his breast pocket, facing the two men nearby. Their voices were coming through loud and clear. Yesterday he had followed the man from the Stettler Building to this location, and then to an apartment on Kentucky Avenue. A check with a gossipy neighbor revealed that Adam Baily and his wife Yolinda lived in apartment 312.

Myron had assumed the coffeehouse was a second home for the nervous man, and the assumption was paying off. Returning here today allowed Myron to continue his surveillance of the man he hoped to blackmail into ending Teddy's life.

Adam continued defending himself. "Just when I found that bag the woman carried, that's when I heard voices and had to leave. There was not time to grab the bag and take it with me." He sipped his coffee. "The dead agent had little time between taking our CD and falling. Two minutes, not more." Adam studied his friend's face. "You searched his body carefully?"

Mario nodded.

"Then our information has to be in that woman's bag, or," he paused, his eyes bright, "it may be with the red-haired one who helped her. He may have found it."

"His name was not in the newspaper story." Mario paused. "Perhaps he also works for the FBI."

"I will find him." Adam's smile gave way to a frown. There had been a man at the elevator in the Stettler Building yesterday. Could it have been the same red-haired man who tried to help the FBI agent? "Hopefully whoever has our CD has not had time to listen beyond the first song. It was wise to encrypt Alliance information after that song played."

"Would the woman not grow suspicious if she finds that recording?" Mario scowled at Adam. "Do you not read the papers? Your visit to her office was discovered."

After an uncomfortable pause, Adam whispered, "I have been making a plan." He leaned toward Mario.

At the next table the man behind the newspaper fiddled with something in his breast pocket, then he leaned forward.

Adam's audience was ready to hear the details of his plan.

When the two friends left the coffeehouse, Myron followed at a distance. It was obvious to him that his ex-wife had something they wanted. Funny how she managed to get her hands on other people's property. He grimaced, remembering the money-laundering records she'd discovered as they separated. That information could put him behind bars for this lifetime and the next.

What he needed were details of the relationship between these men and Teddy. Once he had that he'd be ready to have a serious chat with them.

At a restaurant near the Stettler, Teddy sat with Frances and Gene Ravensworth, enjoying a late lunch. She said, "I didn't realize I was so hungry."

"It's nearly dinnertime," Frances commented, picking up her turkey sandwich.

Gene interrupted. "After that exposé in the paper this morning, I thought we should caution you."

Teddy laughed. "You've done that, Gene; both you and Frances. I am *not* going into hiding."

"When we spoke to the FBI yesterday they indicated you may be in danger because you can identify the man who searched Sam."

"And?" Teddy gave him a puzzled look.

Gene continued. "I think we have to assume he wasn't going through Sam's pockets looking for medical information. The break-in at your office probably means whatever Sam got hold of is still missing."

Teddy nodded. "I've searched through my purchases and there's nothing I didn't buy." She added, "Other than Sam whispering my name, I don't think I'm involved except accidentally. It could just as easily be Connor who ended up with what Sam had. Or perhaps someone in the crowd found it after he fell."

Gene said, "Thanks to the newspaper story, everyone is focused on you having it."

Teddy put her sandwich down and pushed the plate away. "I have a bit of news that answers some of our questions. I went to see that reporter who keeps setting me up as a target."

"What did Bradford have to say for him- or herself?" Gene asked.

"I didn't talk to him, although he was at his desk flying paper airplanes." Teddy smiled at the puzzled expressions across from her. "However, I got a very good look at Mr. Connor Bradford Douglas fiddling away his time as he creates another fairy tale."

"Connor is a reporter?" Gene shook his head. "He's the one writing the *News Telegrapher* stories?"

Teddy nodded. "I have one other bit of news to share." She picked up her sandwich, and then lay it back on the plate. "Myron has been paroled."

"You're kidding!" Gene shook his head. "He may try to make good on his threat to kill you. Tell Brighton about him."

"Thanks to Connor," grimaced Teddy, "Myron won't have any trouble finding me."

While Teddy notified the FBI about the troublesome men in her life, one of them was stretching his long legs across the top of a messy desk at the *News Telegrapher*. He wiggled his bare toes in the orange-checkered flip flops he liked to wear year 'round. A satisfied smile was on his face. He couldn't help himself. What a great series he was running. What luck to be present when a front-page story broke. Favorable comments from fellow reporters arrived hourly. Even competitors were giving him a grudging thumbs-up.

How to spin out the story? He needed another angle, something to hold local interest and keep readers coming back for more. He needed something so sensational the story would be picked up by national news services.

Teddy was his best link to the FBI and whatever plot the dead guy interrupted. If she learned anything, he wanted to be in on it. He thought about his conversation with her the morning someone broke into her office. There was something he had meant to tell her, but the troublesome memory was gone for now. He wiggled his bare toes again and considered various elements he could introduce into tomorrow's story. He swung his legs from the desk. It was time to pay Teddy a visit to see what she'd been doing all day. C. Bradford, crime reporter, left the newsroom whistling.

After the conference at the Corner Coffeehouse ended, Adam drove his white van with *Thompson's Electrical* on the side to the parking lot of a small business advertising *Computerized Signs and Graphics—Magnetics Our Specialty*. Myron followed at a distance, watching as Adam climbed from his truck and entered the shop.

A few minutes later, Adam returned to his van. He entered the back and closed the doors, but when the doors opened again it was obvious he'd changed clothes. With a wave to someone, he left the yard on foot, sprinting down the street.

Myron swung his car into the sign lot, and hurried into the office.

"Be with you in a minute." A man talking on the phone held up one finger and nodded at Myron. "Listen, lady," he said into the receiver. "We'll do another sign, right after you bring the first one back." He listened a minute longer, then added, "Bring it back and we'll take care of it." He slammed the receiver in its cradle and turned to Myron. "What can I do for you?"

"I thought I saw my friend Adam Baily here the other day—in his jogging suit. Is there a certain time I'd be able to catch up with him here?"

The shop owner rose slowly. "There might be. What do you want to see him about?" He sounded suspicious.

Myron immediately sat down. He could see the guy was on the defensive. "That's between Adam and me." He rubbed his right thigh. "I want to hire him to do a job for me 'cause this war injury limits my abilities."

Caught off guard, the shop owner resumed his seat. "Lyle Bascom," he said, reaching out to shake Myron's hand. "Adam's a friend. He parks in our lot because his apartment complex only allows one parking space per tenant. His wife uses the space outside their apartment." Lyle shifted in his chair and added, "He's a runner. He doesn't jog. Don't ever call him a jogger."

Myron remembered to rub his right thigh as he got to his feet. "I guess I'll just catch up with him at his apartment on Kentucky." He reached out to shake hands. "Thanks for your help."

"If it's a sign job you want done, we can do it for you." Lyle fished out a business card and handed it to Myron.

"Thanks," Myron said, eyeing the card. "After I talk with Adam, if I find out the job's something you can handle, then I'll be in touch." He smiled. With his right hand he stuffed the business card into a breast pocket and with his left hand he rubbed his left thigh.

Myron immediately realized his mistake. Awkwardly rubbing *both* thighs, he left the shop.

CHAPTER

8

Teddy searched for her keys, but her thoughts were on Sam Morgan. Had the FBI agent really come out of nowhere to crash into her, or had she noticed him earlier without being aware of it? She tried to recall the events of two days earlier.

Her final purchase had upset the balance of her packages, causing her to stop at an empty park bench to reassemble the load. That done, she'd hurried to the intersection, and when the light changed, crossed the street. Shortly after that, Sam collapsed beside her. Where had he come from?

When no answers came to mind, Teddy shrugged and stuffed files into her briefcase. She grabbed her jacket and discovered her keys in the pocket, but when she looked at them, she remembered the special agent searching Sam's pockets.

She tried to recall the man's features, and when she did, she realized it hadn't been Sam she'd noticed earlier; it had been the man claiming to be a special agent. He'd been sitting near the park's north entrance as she passed by.

Teddy closed her eyes, trying to recall the bearded man in detail. If his attention had been on Sam, where had Sam been at that moment?

If the man on the bench wasn't a special agent, was he, as the FBI suspected, a member of the Delphi Alliance? Had he been waiting in the park because he was part of the information exchange Sam intercepted?

Grabbing her briefcase, Teddy headed for the door. She had thought her real problem was Connor and his duplicity, but it was Sam. She hadn't become involved when Sam bumped her; she'd been involved from the moment she stepped into the park.

If she could remember what she observed, it might help locate Sam's killer. Teddy rushed across the street to the park, ready to retrace her steps.

Using her briefcase as if it were the packages she'd been carrying, she put it on the bench where she'd stopped to rearrange things. What had she noticed as she stood there? She closed her eyes. There had been laughter and conversation around her, and a couple had stepped aside to let a young mother push a stroller down the middle of the path. At a distance skateboarders shouted and exhibited their skills, temporarily blocking a runner who caught up, then passed them. Had she seen anyone as neatly dressed as Sam?

No image came to mind.

Teddy picked up her briefcase and headed toward the park's north entrance. When she came to the bench where the bearded man sat, she settled in approximately the same place. As she'd passed, he'd seemed interested only in his newspaper. But was he? Was there a reason he'd chosen this particular bench? Had he been watching someone?

To his left was the path along which Teddy had come, and to his right, pedestrians waiting for the light to change. A bench across from him hadn't been occupied, and like all benches on that side of the path, it was attached to a garbage can. Behind the bench and garbage can were shrubs and small trees.

What could the man on the bench have seen without turning his head? She held up her briefcase as if it were a newspaper. It blocked her view of the empty bench opposite, the mostly full garbage can beside it, and the shrubs beyond.

She had passed by and joined the group waiting for the light to change. Where was Sam at that moment? It wasn't long after she crossed the street that he'd collapsed at her side. If he crossed the street soon after she did, where had he come from?

Think, she instructed herself. *What did you notice? What did you see, but not put into thoughts or words?*

The blast from a motorist's horn startled her.

There had been a similar burst of frustrated honking as she waited for the light to change that day. She'd glanced briefly in the direction of the sound and saw a jaywalker crossing the street in front of an impatient driver. The jaywalker looked like a businessman running to catch a bus!

Teddy jumped to her feet, staring in the direction of the jaywalker. It was Sam she'd seen.

At that instant the traffic light had changed and she'd crossed the street. A minute or two later Sam collapsed beside her. Somewhere between his jaywalking across the street and bumping against her, Sam intercepted something and received a fatal wound. Where could he have gone in the short time between jaywalking and falling?

Had the man on the bench been waiting for Sam? Had he given him information that got him killed? Was that why he knelt beside her and searched Sam's pockets? Was he trying to retrieve something he'd given Sam, or was he hunting for something Sam stole from him?

Questions tumbled through Teddy's head as she tried to recall events. When she couldn't remember any more, she went to her car and drove home.

A yawn caught her off-guard as she drove into her carport. She stretched and retrieved the CD she'd found in her tote earlier, then walked slowly into the house. She pushed the CD into her player and checked to see if she had a similar recording. When she found one, she set it on her desk to give away. As dinner cooked she called Agent Brighton, to tell him what she'd recalled in the park, adding her discovery of Connor's job as a reporter.

"We'd like you to keep that information to yourself," Brighton said. "We have plans for dealing with Mr. Douglas."

"Plans? Do they have anything to do with alligators?"

Brighton laughed. "Not at the moment."

Teddy hung up. For the time being she'd have to be content only with thoughts of Connor in an alligator-infested pond.

CHAPTER

9

Persistent banging on Teddy's front door interrupted the restful mood being created by *The Sound of Music*. She snapped off her CD player and hurried to the door to look through the peephole. "Connor," she breathed, slowly opening the door, wishing she had an alligator pond for him to swim in.

His hand was raised, ready to bang on her door again.

"Why are you calling on me this time of night?" she asked. "I was getting ready to go to bed."

Connor blinked several times. "You weren't at your office, and when you didn't answer your home phone I got worried about you."

"I don't understand," she said.

"I forgot to warn you about who I saw. Could I come in?"

Remembering the lies he'd told her, she stepped onto her porch, closing the door behind her. He backed away a step or two. "I've had a long, busy day," she said. "What did you want to warn me about?"

He twisted his cap nervously. "I finally remembered what I needed to tell you, and when I couldn't find you, I was afraid something might have happened." He stopped as if that explained everything.

"I'm waiting," she said, more agitated than curious.

"I wanted to tell you about one of the guys in the crowd when Sam died." Connor cleared his throat. "I saw him yesterday when I came for my interview with the FBI. He was coming from the direction of your office, and was out of breath, as if he'd been hurrying!"

An impatient edge crept into Teddy's voice. "You showed up this time of night to tell me the man who said he was a special agent was in the Stettler yesterday?"

"No. Not him. There was another guy in the crowd that day. He was behind you, but facing me. He wore a black running suit and had black curly hair and a mustache. He signaled to the special agent a couple of times. I'm sure they were friends. I told the FBI about them, but I forgot to tell you."

"And," she prompted. She hadn't seen the man he described.

"And he was at the Stettler yesterday. As I got off the elevator he came hurrying from the direction of your office. A guy on crutches yelled to hold the elevator, so when I turned to hold it, that's when I got a good look at the man who'd just gotten on. We recognized each other. I'm sure of it. When I got to your office, you were talking with that attorney and. . . ."

"And I'd just discovered someone ransacked my office."

"Right! I was so excited about your burglary that I forgot to tell you who I'd just seen."

Teddy frowned. "Then the special agent wasn't alone."

Connor shrugged his shoulders. "I don't think so." A long minute passed. "With his friend in your building the next day, and your office ransacked. . . ." He let the sentence hang unfinished. "If the FBI agent really intercepted something, it was still missing yesterday."

"And someone wanted to see if I had it."

"Right. And if the guy searching didn't find it at your office, then the next place to look is here, at your home."

"They could look at *your* place," she shot back. "You were there."

Connor straightened up. "Yeah," he agreed reluctantly. "But there hasn't been any mention of me in the newspaper. Finding me won't be easy."

"Lucky you." Teddy sounded sarcastic.

Connor stared at her. "Are you absolutely sure Sam didn't slip you something?"

"Of course I'm sure!" She opened the door behind her and grabbed her tote, then tipped it upside down, shaking its contents into an empty planter. "See? Makeup, I.D., and money. All mine. Nothing else."

Connor studied her angry expression, then quietly said, "You were the only person close to Sam as he fell."

"That's true, but I had my hands full of packages. You're assuming something we don't *know*," Teddy protested. "We don't know *where* Sam made the intercept or how long after he made it that he showed up beside me."

She was sure now that Sam had less than two minutes to get the information before he was struck down, but she wasn't about to tell Connor.

"It couldn't have been long," Connor said, giving his cap another twist. "He probably found something in the park, then headed back to his office with it."

"You're forgetting that he could have found something miles away, *days* earlier, and the murderers only caught up with him moments before his death. The only things I had with me that day were office supplies and my tote. Both were in my office yesterday so I assume the burglar checked them." She looked at Connor. "If Sam slipped something into my tote, then whoever searched my office has it."

"Maybe," he conceded. "But if. . . ."

"If, if, if," Teddy interrupted. "While we were in the police car, I gave you a business card from the box of cards I had in my tote. If there had been anything unusual in it, something I hadn't put there, don't you think I'd have realized it?"

"We were both pretty upset." Connor adjusted his glasses. "We don't know how big or how small the missing object is. What we do know is that the burglar risked being discovered when he checked your office during the day. Whatever is missing has to be worth the risk."

"You're now on a subject I can discuss! Someone broke into my office because that irresponsible Bradford set me up. Thanks to him, I'm a target for Sam's killers and for any other disturbed individuals roaming Whittington's streets." Her face flushed in anger.

"I left messages for Bradford and his editor," Connor said.

"Really?" Teddy's eyes narrowed to tiny slits.

He continued, "I told them to back off and stop giving out your personal information."

Teddy laughed. "And you expect that to happen just because some anonymous person suggests it?"

Connor shifted his feet nervously. "I told Bradford I was a tough dude and if he didn't write more responsibly, I'd pay him a visit he'd regret."

Teddy didn't reply. If Agent Brighton hadn't told her to keep quiet about Connor's occupation, she'd have lost it. For the moment she envisioned an alligator pond with Connor swimming frantically. She smiled. "Do you know how to swim?" she asked.

He looked puzzled. "Do you think I went too far with Bradford?" he responded. Frown lines creased his forehead.

Calmly, picturing an alligator with Connor caught between its jaws, she said, "I think you didn't go far enough." *How could she believe anything he said?* "I've been wondering what C. Bradford's first name is. Do you think it could be con man? Creep? Crook?"

Connor's face turned red, and he broke into a cold sweat. "I'll keep trying to see him," he said.

"Forget it," she snapped. "I've got more on my mind than a small town reporter pretending he's some big-shot journalist, who. . . ." Teddy searched for words that wouldn't reveal what she knew about Connor. At the moment, he looked like he was having trouble breathing. "Are you all right?" she asked solicitously, barely able to suppress a satisfied smile. "Do you need a drink?" *A cup of hemlock, perhaps?*

Connor wiped his forehead, and shook his head. "No thanks. I'll get going now that I know you're safe. But be careful, won't you?"

"Of course." Teddy opened the door and stepped back into the house. "Keep in touch," she invited insincerely, closing the door, and locking it.

Back in his car, Connor phoned in a small addition to his story in time to meet the evening's deadline. In tomorrow's edition a slain FBI agent would die in the arms of a lovely young woman. It was time to hint at the possibility of dangers from sources unknown. He visualized his headline on page one, above the fold—his name prominently featured in the byline. With luck the series would get him what every reporter wanted—a Pulitzer.

###

"I know where the woman and the red-haired man both live," Adam said later that night. He'd followed Connor from Teddy's house. "That man with red hair visited the woman tonight. They are not strangers. When he left I followed. I can now search his place, too."

"Cool. Nice going," Mario said. "You have everyone's support. But you must remember we are approaching Isaac's deadline. You need to find that CD."

"It is done. When that woman leaves for work tomorrow, I will check out her taste in music." Adam's smile curled his lips. He would save the Alliance's operations, keep Yolinda safe from Isaac's threats, and be a hero among the brotherhood.

But this time, he reminded himself sternly, before he searched the woman's house, he'd first look for escape routes.

###

Teddy was asleep when her bedside phone rang. "Yes?" she mumbled, fumbling with the receiver.

"Are you the Teddy Sanderson who's been in the news recently?" The caller growled his question.

"Who is this?" Teddy asked, sitting up, on the alert.

"Stay out of things, lady, or you'll regret it. There are more of us involved in this than you know."

"Who is this?" Teddy asked again, her heart beating faster. "What are you talking about?"

"I'm the guy who's gonna see that you stay out of our way." The statement was followed by a hollow laugh.

"Are you threatening *me*?"

The line went dead.

Wide awake now, Teddy switched on her bedside lamp and wrote down the caller's message. When she finished, she dialed Agent Brighton's unlisted number.

"Yes?" asked a sleepy voice.

"It's Teddy Sanderson. You said to call if anything unusual happened. Since I've just received a threatening phone call, I thought you'd want to know."

"We put a trace on your phone. It will have started already, but stop by my office in the morning. We'll talk then."

CHAPTER
10

Teddy's frustrations continued in earnest early the next morning. The *News Telegrapher's* front page story recounted her witnessing of the federal agent's murder. It also mentioned events that had taken place in her life including her short marriage to Myron Ratini. An anonymous source being quoted said Sam tried to save the world, a task now in Teddy's hands.

Sam's funeral notice appeared in the sidebar, almost as an afterthought.

Teddy slammed the newspaper on her breakfast table. Connor Bradford Douglas needed to be stopped. If the FBI wouldn't do it; she would find a way.

###

"It has come to my attention, Miss Sanderson," Special Agent Dillard Brighton said, flicking invisible lint from the sleeve of his suit coat, "that you have taken over Sam's attempt to save the world." The seasoned agent looked thoughtful as he met Teddy's angry eyes. He reached out to take her arm. "Let's continue our discussion in my office." He guided her to a small room at the end of the hall.

As they entered, Teddy forced a polite response, "I want you to brief me on laws relating to justifiable homicide." Her eyebrows pinched together under the frown lines covering her forehead.

"Please sit down, Miss Sanderson," Dillard said, waiting until she perched on the edge of a chair. "Was there anything other than Mr. Douglas or your phone call last night that you wanted to talk to me about this morning?"

Teddy took a deep breath. "What did you learn about the caller who threatened me last night?"

"We traced him. His name is Wendell Green and he's already on a watch-list." Dillard studied Teddy's serious face, then picked up his phone, swung his chair around to face the window behind him, and spoke a few quiet words before hanging up. He turned back to Teddy. "I'm concerned about the threat to you. Thankfully, because you agreed to taps on both your home and office phones, we were able to quickly trace that call last night."

"What will happen if I get more calls like that? Or more burglaries? What if that caller shows up at my home some night?"

Before Brighton could answer, there was a sharp rap on his door and a slim young man in a business suit entered. "Miss Sanderson," Agent Brighton pushed his chair back and stood. "This is Special Agent Thomas Heeter. Tom, meet Teddy Sanderson."

The tall, rangy man with wavy chestnut hair and horn-rimmed glasses nodded at Teddy. After shaking her hand in a no-nonsense grip, he pulled up the remaining visitor chair and sat down.

"Tom, Miss Sanderson and I were about to discuss how we're going to protect her." Brighton turned back to Teddy and resumed his seat. "What I'm about to tell you," he said, "is confidential. You are not free to repeat it to anyone, including your friends the Ravensworths. Understood?"

Teddy nodded, a puzzled look on her face.

"As you may have gathered, the intercept Special Agent Morgan made, had to do with our investigation of people moving from malicious mischief into the realm of actual federal crimes. When they do that, stopping them is worth the expense of a full federal investigation."

"I don't understand," Teddy said.

Dillard nodded. "In the past there have been two levels to the schemes focused on damaging infrastructure to various companies. Besides the actual physical damage, there has been an attempt to cause stock values to plummet. Extremists who were once content to chain themselves to trees or lie on highways to block various projects, have moved from mischief into crimes of a federal nature. Since 1990 they've been responsible for thousands of attacks on businesses around the country. We suspect foreign agents may have infiltrated some groups, providing money, membership and media attention."

Agent Brighton stopped talking and studied Tom Heeter. After receiving a nod, Brighton continued. "With help from foreign countries, radical elements in this country have been able to engage in greater damage and disruption of the U.S. economy. The CD we think Sam had in his possession is the first of several errors in the group's scheme."

Teddy leaned back in her chair, studying Agent Brighton. "How does this involve me?"

Brighton continued, "I asked you not to let Connor Douglas know you'd discovered his true identity because we want to feed him misinformation that we hope will help identify Delphi Alliance members. Mr. Douglas doesn't seem to be part of any group. He's simply eager to further his writing career and win awards."

"We need your help," Agent Heeter interjected.

"Me?" Teddy looked first at one man and then at the other. She shrugged her shoulders. "What can I do?"

Dillard Brighton frowned. "Unfortunately you picked the wrong place and the wrong time to show up. You also stepped forward to help a dying man, and by doing so, you became a party to our investigations."

"And Connor?" Her voice was tight in her throat.

"He too was in the wrong place at the wrong time." Agent Brighton looked from his co-worker back to Teddy. "Special Agent Heeter will spend some personal time with you to cut down on opportunities for someone to hurt you."

Teddy's head snapped in Agent Brighton's direction, her eyes wide. "What do you mean by *personal time*?"

Dillard studied the young woman's face. "Your friend Gene Ravensworth assured us you have no," he hesitated, "...no special man in your life at the moment. Therefore, Agent Heeter won't complicate any relationships you have. That *is* true, isn't it?"

"Why don't you spell it out for me, Agent Brighton? What do you mean by *personal time?*"

"Lucky you," Tom Heeter said, extending his hand, a solemn expression on his face. "Shake hands with your new boyfriend."

Teddy returned to her office, surprised at the room's temperature. The unexpected coolness startled her, and she paused at the thermostat, noting it was set for seventy-two degrees. Clearly, the room was colder than that. Shivering again, she turned the dial to seventy-five and made a mental note to report the problem to the building superintendent.

When she saw her phone's message light blinking, she hurried to her desk. The first call had been from Frances, inviting her to dinner on Saturday. "We'll celebrate your first week in business as a Girl Friday," the familiar voice said.

The second call came from Connor, his voice loud and angry. Teddy held the receiver away from her ear. "I'm calling to ask if you've seen Bradford's latest column. I'm going to sit at that reporter's desk until he shows up. Then I'll punch him in the nose. I'll talk to you later, probably from jail."

Teddy stabbed a finger on *delete*, erasing that bit of fiction.

The third call was from the building superintendent introducing himself as Donald Kennedy. He said fourth floor occupants were complaining about the lack of heat and he would take care of the problem as soon as possible. He sounded apologetic.

The last call, from a woman named Thelma Rasmussen, asked about employment opportunities. "When I was in the Stettler today, I noticed your *open for business* sign. I have clerical experience. Please consider me for any openings you might have." The woman hesitated. "I need to get out of the house." Another pause; longer this time. "I would be willing to volunteer my time until you can afford to pay me, if money's an issue." The woman added her name and phone number to her message.

Teddy jotted down the information. If Thelma Rasmussen really meant she'd be willing to work cheap, employing her might benefit both of them. Teddy made an appointment to meet with Thelma the next day. After that, she began calling towing companies. It was important to find the owner of a blue rig with a bull-bar bumper before another attempt was made on William Smith's life.

On the fifth floor of the Stettler Building, Agent Brighton rubbed the back of his hand across his forehead, then said, "Sam was part of the team concentrating on eco-terrorists. He hoped to locate and intercept communications between various terrorist groups. His death seems to indicate he may have been successful." Dillard frowned as he paused. "We need to learn where the exchange took place."

"Sam's wife said she gave him a lead she picked up from her job as a parole officer." Tom's fingers interlocked behind his head. "What I don't understand is why Sam didn't leave any information. He must have stumbled on something and had to move so fast he didn't have time for notes."

"Thanks to Miss Sanderson's recall of events, we know less than ten minutes went by between Sam leaving his office and when he collapsed. We're checking his phone line to see if a call triggered a move on his part."

"The big question is, if he intercepted a drop, what happened to it?"

Dillard nodded. "Sanderson thinks he recognized her. We just don't know how soon that happened, or if it played a part in what happened next."

"I see what you're getting at," Tom mused. "If he realized he was in trouble and saw someone he recognized, he might pass the information to them."

"Exactly. But she insists he didn't give her anything." Dillard studied the pile of papers on his desk, then reached out to pull them toward him. "Ravensworth thinks highly of her, so I don't think she's lying."

"It may be she hasn't recognized whatever Sam gave her," Tom replied.

Dillard began sorting papers. "In any case, she may be in danger. If we're dealing with Isaac Yrask and his accomplices, then we're going to have to be extra careful. Someone has already searched Sanderson's office. If they didn't find what they were looking for there, they'll search her home next."

Tom Heeter nodded. "And that's where I come in?"

"That's exactly where you come in," Dillard agreed. "She may know more than she realizes. If that's the case, you need to help her figure it out." Brighton watched the uncertainty on Tom's face. He gave the young agent a weak smile. "Try not to have too much fun at the agency's expense."

"What an assignment," Tom said, trying to look stern, but failing. He smiled as he left the room.

Dillard turned his attention back to the work on his desk. "Assigned to escort a pretty young witness. What a challenge." He sighed and began sorting papers.

CHAPTER
11

Don Kennedy, the Stettler's maintenance superintendent, sipped cold coffee and from time to time ran nervous fingers over his bald head. A phone conversation with a friend from his less structured past troubled him.

Preserving forests and wetlands had been Don's passion decades earlier, but he was married now, with a responsible job. It didn't pay a lot, but it suited him, and it took advantage of his knack for fixing things. He liked being in charge of a building with the FBI in it. "I'm part of National Security," he would brag after a drink or two in the evening.

He pushed a stack of papers to the back of his desk just as a timid knock sounded on his door. Before he could stand up, a dumpling of a woman with two metal canes entered. A small pack was strapped to her back.

"Hi Donnie," she greeted, breathing heavily as she removed the small pack. "You forgot your lunch, so I thought I'd drop it off on my way to the doctor."

Don jumped to his feet to get the sack lunch. "I could have eaten this for supper. I don't like causing you to make extra trips." He gave her an affectionate peck on the top of her head. "You're too good to me."

Ella laughed and returned his kiss. She was short, plump and had a round face, while Don was tall, slender and the only hair on his head formed a small mustache and thick eyebrows.

"Do you have time for a cup of coffee?" He motioned to a fresh pot still brewing.

She shook her head. "It looks like you're getting ready for a meeting."

He nodded. "I'm expecting Bob Rasmussen to drop by. Remember him?" The man they'd known as Raz had set up today's meeting.

Ella frowned. "I've never liked that man, Donnie. I know you worked with him on your environmental projects, but...." She shook her gray head. "There's something about him. He's so," she paused, "... so radical."

Her husband laughed. "We were all radical in the old days."

A knock on the door interrupted. "That might be him," Don whispered, moving to the door to open it.

"I got here faster than I expected," said the heavy-set man as he stepped into Don's office. He looked like he needed a shave.

"It's good to see you again, Raz." The men shook hands. "You remember Ella, don't you?"

"Of course." Raz nodded at Don's wife.

"Before you two get started on old times, I'll skedaddle," Ella said. "I have a doctor's appointment." She met her husband's eyes and added, "See you this evening, dear. Don't be late." With that, she made her way slowly out of the office.

"I promise," Don called out before turning to his friend. "Coffee, Raz?"

The visitor shook his head. "I won't be staying that long."

Don filled his own cup and sat down. As soon as he did, his guest launched into the proposition he'd hinted at on the telephone. Don listened carefully. It seemed to him that the group he'd once belonged to was headed for trouble. Where members once tied themselves to trees and used sit-ins to block road construction projects, their recent activities had become destructive.

Raz continued, "Besides planting a bug in a thermostat on the fourth floor, we want you to do some specialized work in those FBI offices."

"I can't do that," Don burst out. "Breaking into offices on the fifth floor would end my career. I have Ella to consider. I can't do anything that would send me to prison."

Bob Rasmussen lit a cigarette, but said nothing as he blew smoke into the air.

"And there's my retirement," Don added, fidgeting in his chair. "At my age, I can't put that in jeopardy."

Raz's cigarette smoke curled around Don's worried face. Finally Raz broke the silence. "Is there anything I can say that will convince you to help us? You believed in our cause once upon a time." His voice was smooth and persuasive, but his eyes had narrowed.

Don sighed. "That was then, Raz. Things are different for me now. I still believe in the group's cause, but not in the way they're handling it. I can plant the bug in Sanderson's office but count me out on the FBI job. Every inch of the fifth floor has surveillance cameras." He studied the man opposite him. "I know I'm the man with the keys, but I can't take part in activities involving the FBI."

Raz got slowly to his feet, flicking cigarette ashes to the floor.

"It isn't that I don't want to help when I can," Don added. "I turned off the heat to the fourth floor as you asked, but I'd be the first one suspected of the job you want done on five. Then what, spend the rest of my life in the slammer?"

Raz reached across the desk and dropped his cigarette in Don's coffee cup. It sputtered briefly. "Forget about the bug," he growled. "I'll take care of it myself. Turn the fourth floor's heat back on in thirty minutes and then forget we ever had this conversation."

Don Kennedy watched as Raz disappeared down the hall. When he was finally out of sight, Don glanced at the discarded cigarette floating in his coffee cup. He could feel a headache coming on.

The driver of a white van parked on the quiet residential street climbed out. *People are at work*, thought Adam. *It makes my job easier.*

His white coveralls were clean and professional-looking, and advertised *Thompson's* in black lettering over the breast pocket. A magnetic sign on the side of the truck said *Thompson's Electrical, We Light Up Your Life*.

Adam hooked a tool belt around his waist, grabbed a red toolbox, and crossed the street to Teddy Sanderson's front porch. He looked business-like knocking on her door. There was no answer, but he hadn't expected one. He knocked again, then folded a blank piece of paper and tucked it into a crack between the screen and its frame. A serviceman had merely left a note that he'd been there and would call again.

To allay suspicions of watchful neighbors, Adam took a few steps toward his truck, then stopped and turned back. Let them think he'd had a new idea or that someone called him. He followed a path to Teddy's backyard where he put on gloves before pulling a screwdriver from his tool belt. He plunged the screwdriver into the space between the screen door and its frame, and wiggled it until he'd unhooked the latch. As he put the screwdriver away he entered Teddy's kitchen and listened for sounds. When the only one he heard was the quiet ticking of a clock, he checked out possible escape routes. Feeling secure, he crossed to the dining room and inspected it. Beyond, in the living room, he could see the front entry and a hall that probably led to bedrooms. A desk stood beside a bookcase. On a top shelf of the bookcase he could see a collection of CDs. He hurried to the bookcase ready to search for *The Sound of Music,* but when he reached the desk, he found the CD he wanted on top of it. A feeling of relief washed over Adam. His family was saved.

He grabbed the CD, checked to make sure the case wasn't empty, then slid it into a deep pocket in his coveralls. He hurried back through the kitchen, and with a sigh of relief picked up his toolbox, and headed out the back door. He'd taken only two steps outside when a deep growl startled him.

He froze. He hated dogs. They always looked ready to attack. He measured the distance from where he stood to his truck, but it was too far to risk running. He took a tentative step and the dog growled again. Slowly Adam turned toward the sound.

A black and brown German shepherd stood on the other side of a chain link fence. The dog's lips were curled back to expose sharp white teeth. The growling came from deep in the dog's throat. Adam gulped, checking the fence for openings. When he saw none, he risked hurrying to his truck. The barking dog followed along the length of its fenced yard.

Adam dropped his toolbox in the back of the truck, and unbuckled his tool belt as he climbed in the front seat. He put the truck in gear and glanced one last time at the barking dog. As he pulled away, he became aware of a curtain fluttering in a window behind the dog.

Teddy glanced at the wall clock to confirm lunch time. She put on her coat, grabbed her purse, and switched off the office lights. Just as she reached for the door knob, her phone rang. She hurried back to the desk and leaned across it to grab the receiver. "Girl Friday, Sanderson speaking."

"Hi, Teddy. It's me, Tom."

"Tom?" She sounded puzzled.

"Teddy! It's me, your boyfriend! Hey, my feelings are hurt."

"Oh," she exclaimed. "I'm sorry. I was thinking about something else."

"I'm calling to see if we can meet for lunch, or if that doesn't work, let's have dinner. Your choice."

The eagerness in Tom's voice made her uncomfortable. This so-called *relationship* needed to be kept on a business-like basis except when absolutely necessary. "I guess we could meet for lunch," she replied slowly, "but I have to be back here in an hour."

"Since time's a problem, let's meet at your place. It's close. I'll bring a pizza."

"Okay, but no anchovies. Do you know where I live?" She suddenly remembered they were supposed to know each other very well.

"Of course I know where you live. I'll see you in a few minutes."

Teddy frowned and put the receiver down. She was starting a new business, and had clients with important problems. What she didn't need was a pretend boyfriend, or, for that matter, an ex-husband running loose. A twinge of concern gnawed at her. In the past even a restraining order hadn't kept Myron from trying to kill her. Would things be any different after four years?

A noise startled her and she whirled around to find a tall, heavy-set man standing behind her. She gripped the edge of the desk for support. "May I help you?" She tried to sound calm, but her heart raced. *How long had he been there? How much had he overheard?*

"Sorry if I startled you, miss. I'm checking thermostats on this floor." The stranger pulled a screwdriver from his belt and began removing the casing from her thermostat. "I didn't see any lights on in here so I thought you'd gone to lunch. I decided to start working at this end of the hall."

"I remember. You phoned earlier. I just didn't hear you come in."

He held up a silver key. "I used my passkey."

"Remind me of your name, please."

"Don Kennedy."

She nodded. "I hope you get the heat back on. I really shivered in here this morning." She gathered her things and gave him an uncertain smile. "Please lock up when you leave."

"Of course," he replied.

Teddy felt uneasy having someone in her office when she wasn't there. All the way to the basement parking garage she worried about the man in her office. He was more unkempt than she expected of a superintendent at the Stettler, and that troubled her. As she unlocked her car door, a thought occurred. *What was a new FBI boyfriend for if it wasn't to check on repairmen?* Relaxing somewhat, she drove home, ready for a meeting with a man too handsome for his own good.

CHAPTER

12

Bob Rasmussen chuckled as he tightened the last screw on Teddy's thermostat. With the tiny piece of electronic equipment he'd installed, every word she uttered would be overheard. To make sure, he placed an even smaller device in her telephone, then turned out the lights and stepped from her office. He almost collided with Connor Douglas.

"She's at lunch," Raz announced, pulling the door shut behind him. He locked it and jiggled the knob to make sure.

"Did she say when she'd be back?" Connor's face betrayed his disappointment.

"Naw. Superintendents aren't favored with that kind of information." Raz moved toward the stairs just beyond Teddy's office.

"How do I know you're really the superintendent?" Connor asked.

Raz whirled around. "Who the hell do you think *you* are?" He stood half a foot taller than Connor and outweighed him by at least sixty pounds. He took a step toward the nearsighted young man.

"I'm with the FBI," Connor improvised, holding his ground. "Show me your identification."

Raz sniggered. "You're about as much FBI as I am."

While Connor struggled for a response, Raz headed once more for the stairwell. Behind him, Connor's camera made a tiny clicking sound as it flashed.

Tom Heeter stood on Teddy's front porch balancing a pizza box in one hand and a briefcase in the other. He wore blue jeans and a sweater, and his horn-rimmed glasses had been pushed to the top of his head. "Hi, there," he greeted as she came toward him.

"Hi, yourself. What happened to the business suit?"

"This outfit is my casual dress."

She nodded and opened the screen, ready to unlock her front door when a piece of paper fluttered to the porch. She bent to retrieve it. "That's funny. It's blank on both sides."

Tom looked over her shoulder. "Lay it on the pizza box and open the door. It's cold out here."

Teddy put the paper on the box and unlocked the door.

"Why don't you set the table while I wash up?" Tom handed her the pizza and raising his index finger to his lips, signaled her to keep quiet. He removed a small plastic bag from one pocket and maneuvered the blank paper she'd found into it. Then he tucked the bag in his pocket, and whispered, "We'll see what the fingerprint guys come up with."

Teddy nodded, put the pizza on the dining room table and moved into the kitchen, calling out for beverage preferences.

"Cola of some kind," Tom answered, taking an unusual piece of equipment from his briefcase. With it he moved quickly through her house. When he returned to the dining area, he said, "Your place is clean, except for the bug we put in your phone."

"That's a relief?"

He put his equipment away and sat down to help himself to a slice of pizza.

"I can't believe anyone other than my ex-husband cares about what's going on in my house," Teddy said, helping herself to the pizza.

"Fill me in on this ex-husband of yours."

Teddy swallowed first. "He was convicted of manslaughter and sentenced to ten years, but after only four, he's back on the street."

"I'll need a picture so I can tell when he's around. But for now, let's stick to the reason I'm here." He studied the young woman across from him. "If the department's assumption is correct and Sam got hold of something from a group of radicals, then the break-in at your office probably means whoever he took it from thinks you have it."

"I can thank Connor's stories for that."

"If your burglars didn't find what they were looking for in your office, then the paper at your front door may mean you've had a visitor here." He handed her a napkin and pointed at her chin. "Check the tomato paste, then see if anything in the house is disturbed, or missing."

Teddy patted her chin; locking eyes with him. "Food first. I'm starved."

Tom studied her face. "What if the paper we found means you've had an intruder and it was your ex-husband?"

With trembling hands Teddy pushed away from the table and dashed through various rooms. "Nothing seems out of place," she reported, breathing heavily. "In the past when Myron broke in, he cut electrical cords in half and killed my cat. I think if he'd been in here this time, he'd have done something obvious, like leaving a bomb in the middle of the table."

"Does he want to kill you?"

She nodded. "He's tried twice that I know of." She glanced at her watch and sat down again. "We need to finish lunch so I can get back to the office."

For a while they ate in silence. "Why does your ex want to kill you?" Tom asked.

Teddy remained silent for a minute. "At first, I thought it was because he didn't want the divorce. But later, after I found his personal computer files among my papers, and the subject of money laundering came up. . . ."

"Whoa!" Tom said. "Money laundering? That means IRS wants him."

"You've got it. And because I'm the one who opened the door to them. . . ."

Tom nodded. "I see." He gave her an appraising look. "Dillard wants me to provide you with security. Crimes require opportunity, and we don't want you to be viewed as being vulnerable. I'm here to cut down on opportunities."

"How long will this charade last?"

"There's no way to predict that, but it shouldn't interfere too much with your business." He studied her face. "I don't intend to take advantage of the situation as I role play, if that's worrying you."

"I guess that's good news." She smiled.

"The faster we get this case wrapped up, the sooner everyone can get back to their real lives. I know Dillard asked if Sam passed you anything, but I'm asking again."

Teddy shook her head. "He didn't."

"Let's assume he wouldn't tap you on the shoulder and hand you something. Let's say he slipped it to you as he fell. What were you carrying?"

"I had office supplies in plastic bags. They were in my office, and whoever searched it the next morning, unwrapped them."

"Were there any pockets on your clothes or a gaping handbag?"

"I didn't think about coat pockets." Teddy hurried to the hall closet and removed a red raincoat. She searched its pockets, retrieving only a pair of black gloves and a note with Connor's personal information.

"How about your handbag?"

"I had a tote with me, but I emptied it when Connor asked about it last night. It was also in my office when someone broke in. I assume they searched it."

"I see," he replied. "Okay. The next thing I want to caution you about is what you say about the two of us. By now the records at your high school should show you and I were there at the same time, until my family moved away during my sophomore year. You and I are currently renewing an old relationship, with a lot of unknowns."

Teddy said, "Will you be able to help me if I have requests?"

"Probably." He studied her face. "Did you have something in mind?"

Teddy nodded.

"Go ahead."

"When I talked to you on the phone an hour ago, my back was to the hall door because I had been headed out when the phone rang. A man entered the office behind me, so silently I didn't know he was there until I turned around. He didn't knock or say anything. He just came in. When I hung up the phone, there he stood."

"Did he say why he was there?"

"My office didn't have heat this morning. He said he was there to fix the problem, but the way he entered made me nervous. I also thought he looked more casual than a building superintendent should look. He needed a shave. Could you check on him, please?"

Tom carried their dishes to the kitchen sink while Teddy put leftover pizza in the refrigerator. "Did he tell you his name?"

"Don Kennedy."

"That's the building superintendent. I'm assuming you hadn't met him yet." He watched Teddy shake her head. "I suggest you get acquainted with various staff members in the building."

"Give me a break. I haven't had time. This is still my first week trying to set up a new business in a new location."

Tom smiled. "If you're ready to return to work, let's go. I want to sweep your office for bugs. I'll check out your visitor after Sam's funeral."

"You don't need to take me to work."

"I expect to be taking you to and from work most days."

"Will you accompany me on surveillance trips?" She laughed.

"If it comes to that." Tom headed for the front door. "I'll get my suitcase, and then we'll head back to your office."

"Suitcase?" Teddy's eyes opened wide.

Tom nodded. "Which bedroom do you want me to use?"

CHAPTER

13

Adam hurried through the Corner Coffeehouse to Mario's table, waving a CD. "I got it," he whispered with a smile.

"Stop the waving and sit down," Mario hissed, his fingers shielding his mouth. "Are you sure it's ours? Did you listen?"

"I came directly here." Adam frowned. "There was no listening time."

At that moment Mario noticed a man with dark curly hair enter the coffee shop. He bought a cup of coffee, then sat at a table close to Mario's and began fiddling with what looked like a pack of cigarettes in his pocket. Mario had noticed him before, always seeming to show up soon after Adam arrived. *Could he be with the FBI? Was he following Adam?*

"Must I tell you everything?" Mario whispered, nervously tapping his fingers as he watched the stranger out of the corner of his eye. "We are too often like this." His hand drew circles in the air. "This is not what Isaac wants."

Adam put the CD in his pocket. "I will listen, and then...."

"And then you will get us again on schedule."

Adam nodded and in a low voice asked, "Will exploding devices be delivered to the same place?"

Mario noted the man at the next table suddenly edging forward in his chair. *Perhaps the time has come to make changes.* He whispered to Adam, "We will never meet like this again. You understand?"

Adam patted his pocket. "When I am sure this is ours, I will give it to the local leader. Isaac will be pleased."

Teddy unlocked her office door and was greeted by a wave of warm air. "Thank goodness. It's fixed." She turned to Tom, "It looks like the repairman really was...."

He laid his finger against her lips. "...taking care of your heating problems. It's really comfortable in here, but since I have to find an apartment and a job, I'll be on my way. Wish me luck and send me off with a goodbye kiss."

He could see his comment startled her. With a smile he kissed his index finger with a smooching sound, then moved to her desk and opened his briefcase. He removed the bug detector and walked around the room, checking for listening devices. In a moment he pointed to the thermostat, and soon after, to the telephone.

"Oh baby," he breathed softly, standing close to the thermostat as he invented a scenario. "When you kiss me like that, I go crazy."

Teddy nodded her understanding. "That's just the way I want you—breathing hard and a little crazy. Now get out of here so I can finish my work."

Tom moved to her desk and on a blank sheet of paper wrote, *this number reaches me, twenty-four/seven.* He jotted a series of numbers on the paper. *Memorize this, and watch what you say until I see if the bugging is ours or theirs. Okay?* He waited for her to agree. "Enough," he said, and pointed at the phone number he'd written down.

"Okay," she whispered, thumping the side of her head.

He folded the paper and put it in his pocket. "I'll see you at five. How about another kiss for the road?"

"Out," she said, laughing. "Find an apartment. You will *not* be sleeping at my house tonight."

"Spoil sport," Tom said, checking his watch. He picked up his briefcase and moved to the thermostat to whisper, "I'll bet real money that I *will* be sleeping at your house tonight."

###

Teddy spent the afternoon talking to towing companies. They assured her that all their trucks were identifiable and had license plates. That meant she'd be sticking close to Sally Anne until the man with the bull bar winch bumper showed up. Teddy was still making phone calls at four-thirty when a light tap sounded on the office door and Tom walked in. The solemn expression on his face reminded her that he'd just attended Sam Morgan's funeral.

"Give me a minute to get my things gathered," she said. "Any luck finding an apartment?"

"I think so, but I'd like you to check it out before we go to dinner."

Teddy collected her purse and coat, and followed Tom to his car.

"The bugs aren't ours," he reported quietly as they buckled their seat belts and entered traffic. "They were probably installed while we ate lunch. Brighton is checking on the building's superintendent. Meanwhile, stay clear of him and remember not to talk about Sam Morgan or anything else regarding that case. Somebody either thinks you know something or they want to make sure you don't." He glanced at Teddy sitting in stony silence, her blue eyes staring ahead unblinking.

She finally said, "Can't you remove the devices? People come to me expecting their problems to be confidential."

"We discussed that, but Brighton thinks it's best not to tip our hand to whoever's listening. Kennedy may turn out to be a dedicated part of the Alliance, or he may just be an unwitting member. Just watch what you say."

"Okay," Teddy whispered, still staring out the window.

"Are you all right?" Tom asked.

She ignored the question. "Was the house hunting you mentioned just something to say for the listening devices?"

"Not at all." He made a sharp right turn onto Canyon Street, and after a few minutes parked in front of a well-tended apartment building. They left the car and climbed the stairs to the second floor where he produced a key to unlock a door.

Teddy stepped into the apartment. "It's charming," she said, noting personal items on a table. "Have you moved in already?"

"Not exactly," Tom responded. "It's a former safe house. Since I needed a place to which interested parties could tail me, this is it."

"Amazing," Teddy said.

"Take this." Tom handed her a key. "It will get you in here if you ever feel uncomfortable going to your home or to your office."

She looked up. "You don't waste time softening scary ideas, do you? You just blurt things out without considering how you might be terrifying me."

"Sorry, but if keeping you terrified is the way to keep you safe, then that's what I'll do. You're in the real world now. *My* world. And my job is to keep you safe. Your job," he added with a smile, "is to pay attention to what I say."

"Does that mean you have new instructions for me?"

He nodded. "Until things settle down, we'll be spending all of our free time together. From tonight on, I'll be sleeping at your place or we'll be sleeping here, so pack a suitcase when you get home."

After dinner Tom and Teddy settled down at Teddy's for the evening, having worked out ways to share the one bathroom. When the phone rang, Teddy grabbed it. "Hello?" she said.

Laughter greeted her, and then, "I see you've got my replacement lined up."

It was the voice Teddy dreamed about when she had nightmares. She signaled to Tom to listen in.

"Spending the night, is he?" Myron continued. "I bet you thought I wouldn't know what you were up to. Well don't get too comfortable with the new guy, Babe. Accidents happen." The line went dead.

"Your ex?" Tom asked.

Teddy nodded. "He's not supposed to contact me." She was shaking.

"We have him on tape," Tom said, referring to the recording device the FBI had installed. "If he calls again, you'll have proof he didn't forget and call once. They'll put him back in prison for six more years."

Teddy began pacing. "I wish Myron was still in prison."

"Why did you marry him," Tom asked.

"We were in high school together. My parents died during my last year, leaving me with no family. Myron's family consisted of an uncle, so in a way, we formed a new family when we married. It's lonely when you haven't anyone to share your life with."

It was a ringing phone that woke Teddy the next morning, but before she could answer it, the ringing stopped. She could tell Tom was on the line so she waited quietly. After a few minutes he came to her bedroom door. "I have an emergency to deal with. You'll need to drive yourself to work this morning. I'll get in touch later."

"What's going on?" she called out, but without answering, he hurried out of the house. Teddy dressed quickly, stuffed the morning newspaper into her briefcase, and drove to the Stettler. She turned into the entrance for the basement garage, but was stopped almost immediately. An armed guard approached her car window. He asked her name and checked it against a list.

"I'm sorry, Miss Sanderson," he said. "You'll have to make other parking arrangements today. There's been an accident and until I hear otherwise, no one's allowed down here."

"What kind of accident," Teddy asked. *Was this what Tom's phone call had been about?*

The guard ignored her question. "Keep moving," he said, motioning her to turn around.

Teddy finally found a parking space a block from the Stettler. When she hurried back, she was surprised to see police everywhere. She identified herself to an officer, and was finally permitted to climb the stairs to her floor. It appeared that the elevators were off limits. When she stepped from the stairwell, she was greeted by one of the younger attorneys from the Booker and Ravensworth offices.

"We haven't met yet," he said, extending his hand to shake hers. "I'm Jed Baxter, one of the attorneys across the hall from you. Did they tell you what happened last night?"

She shook her head. "I only know there's been some kind of accident and they won't let me park in the garage or use the elevators."

"The morning paper had some of the news," Jed replied. "They finally took you off page one and put you on six." He smiled.

"I didn't look at the paper this morning," Teddy said, key out, ready to unlock her door. "Who's on page one?"

"Our building superintendent."

"Mr. Kennedy? What did he do?"

"He died."

Teddy's key dropped to the floor, and she stared at Jed. *The building superintendent is dead? The man Tom and I suspected of planting listening devices in my office has died?* "What happened?" she asked.

"He apparently fell down an elevator shaft. That's why the police won't allow anyone to park in the basement or use the elevators. They're questioning everyone who was in the building last night. The rumor is that Kennedy's death may not be an accident."

The color left Teddy's face.

Jed retrieved her key from the floor and handed it to her. "I didn't mean to upset you. I only meant to bring you up-to-date. We'll know more after the police talk to everyone." He paused, adding, "Can you believe it? A possible murder in a building with the FBI on the top floor?" He hurried off.

Teddy brushed across her eyes, then jabbed her key into the slot twice before the lock turned. She stepped unsteadily into her office and closed the door. Alone, she settled in her chair. She wanted to call Tom, but she couldn't do that on a bugged telephone, and she certainly couldn't talk to Frances. She pulled out her cell phone and punched in Tom's secure number. No answer. In frustration she reached for the *News Telegrapher* she'd tucked in her briefcase and turned to page six.

Connor's story of Sam Morgan spoke of Sam having given his life in an effort to stop the Delphi Alliance. The story included a picture of a tall man, his back to the camera as he entered the stairwell next to Teddy's office. Connor promised that in a later story the mystery man would be revealed as *The Face of Evil*, set on destroying the country.

Teddy stared at the picture. There was a good possibility the man in Connor's picture was the one who let himself into her office, saying he was Don Kennedy. She turned to page one to read about the superintendent's death, and stared at a smiling face she had never seen before.

If the dead man was Don Kennedy, the building superintendent, then who was the man she'd met yesterday who said *he* was Don Kennedy?

###

One hour and a pot of strong coffee later, Teddy put aside the newspaper. She was just organizing folders when Jed Baxter stepped into the office. "Mr. Booker sent you some additional work," he said, handing her a stack of papers, "and I'm supposed to pick up whatever you've already finished."

Teddy handed him the folders she'd been organizing. "Did everyone get their heat back on before Mr. Kennedy died?"

"Sure. As soon as he fixed the master control in the basement, the heating problem was solved. He did that early yesterday."

"Didn't he do something to your thermostat?" she asked.

"No. The problem was caused by a malfunction of the master control downstairs."

Teddy stared at Jed. *The man pretending to be the superintendent used the lack of heat as an excuse to enter my office,* she thought. *Did he steal the key he used from the superintendent and then kill him?*

"The investigators think they know what happened," Jed said. "Kennedy briefed the night crew at the usual time, and they assumed he went home when he finished.

"At seven, a late crew member arrived and noticed Kennedy's car in its regular space, but didn't comment on it because he discovered problems with the elevator. It kept stopping between the basement and the first level. He put an *out of order* sign on it and climbed the stairs to work on his regularly assigned jobs.

"Mrs. Kennedy called at seven fifteen asking about Don's schedule because he hadn't arrived home yet. Not knowing his car was still in the garage, the man who took that call told her Kennedy left at the usual time.

"When crew members finished sweeping the parking garage, they decided to investigate the problem with the elevator. They pried open the door to the shaft and found Kennedy's body. Crime scene investigators think he was pushed into the shaft when the elevator was on a higher floor. They said opening an elevator door when the elevator isn't on that floor is nearly impossible. It takes a very strong person, and Kennedy wasn't that strong."

"Are the police ruling it a homicide?" Teddy's phone rang and she reached for it.

Jed nodded. "I'll talk to you later when I get more details. That work I handed you needs to be done before quitting time today."

Teddy nodded and picked up the receiver. "Girl Friday, Sanderson speaking."

"Did I call at a bad time," Tom asked.

"Not if you're inviting me to lunch."

"Perfect. I'll pick you up at noon. Wait in front of the building. It'll save time."

Teddy began work on the reports Jed had delivered, and was nearly finished when she glanced at the clock. Almost noon. Within minutes she stood in front of the Stettler, waiting for Tom. *First Sam Morgan is murdered, and now the building superintendent. Are their deaths connected? Who'll be next?*

"Get in," Tom called when his Camry pulled up to the curb.

She slid in. "Donald Kennedy is not the man who installed the listening devices in my office," she announced, buckling her seat belt. "That man was heavy-set, and needed a shave. Kennedy was slender."

"Damn." Tom grabbed his cell phone and hit the speed dial. "Dilly, we've underestimated these guys. Get a crew to Teddy's office. See if you can lift prints from her thermostat. Whoever put devices in her office impersonated Kennedy."

"The plot thickens," Teddy said, as Tom ended his call.

"The man impersonating Kennedy was probably an Alliance member," he said.

"He used a key to get in, so he must have gotten it from the real Mr. Kennedy. Do you think that's why Kennedy was murdered?"

CHAPTER

14

After lunch, Tom took Teddy back to her office in time for her interview with Thelma Rasmussen.

"I hope I'm the only one applying for a job," Thelma began as she entered Teddy's office. The forty-year-old wore no makeup and had twisted her hair into a limp ponytail. Her bulky, flat-heeled shoes could have belonged to her husband.

"Sit down, Mrs. Rasmussen," Teddy said, indicating her client chair.

"I had my twins late in life," Thelma continued, still standing. "I thought I'd go nuts before they got old enough to go to school." She took a deep breath. "But now that they're in school and I have free time, I'm bored. I want to feel productive again."

"Please sit down, Mrs. Rasmussen, and catch your breath. Then tell me about your office skills."

"Of course." Thelma thumped down in the chair and inhaled deeply. "Before the twins arrived, I worked as an assistant in an office. I operated computers, or ran errands, that sort of thing. Since then I've been a secretary and treasurer for my church. I can't run a lot of errands anymore because I injured my foot. I need a job where I'm at a desk most of the day."

Teddy said, "I see. What kind of salary did you have in mind?"

"The salary isn't important; I just want out of my house." Thelma ducked her head, then mentioned an amount below minimum wage, adding, "But less than that would be okay, too."

"How can you afford to work for so little?" Teddy asked.

"How can I afford to stay cooped up at home is the better question. Why don't I work for three months, at the minimum wage? After that time we can discuss my salary, or, if you decide to let me go, we shake hands and I look for another job."

Teddy nodded and handed employment forms to Thelma. "Please fill these out. I'll try to get back to you with a decision sometime this weekend."

"I could start as early as Monday," Thelma said as she began filling out the forms. "You're a life saver. I feel like hugging you."

Teddy looked startled. "How about just shaking hands?"

After Thelma left, Teddy finished sorting and cross-referencing the assignments she'd been given. After that, she hurried to Sally Anne's hair solon.

"Back so soon?" Sally Anne asked, fitting a cape around Teddy's neck and shoulders. "Weren't you here just two days ago?"

"My new boyfriend is taking me to meet his folks," Teddy invented. "I want my hair a little shorter. I think I'll look more glamorous."

"Let's give it a try," Sally Anne replied as they walked to the shampoo bowl. There was no further conversation until the women headed back to Sally Anne's station. "I'm assuming this boyfriend isn't the guy you were contemplating doing away with." She combed Teddy's hair, and then began clipping it.

"The guy who needs to breathe his last was only an acquaintance, not a boyfriend."

"I notice your use of past tense. Does that mean something's happened to him?"

"I wish. He's told so many lies about me that I'm getting crank calls from people I don't even know."

"That's serious," Sally Anne said, turning on her curling iron. "No wonder you were upset. Doing away with him might be considered self-defense."

"I like to think of it as justifiable homicide," Teddy said. "I like the sound of that." Looking in the mirror, she added, "I also like what you're doing to my hair."

"You'll be more glamorous with wisps teasing the edge of your face, instead of being pulled away from it."

"Pulling my hair back worked when I used to go four-wheeling."

"Wow! Off-road four-wheeling? I'm a big fan. If you're interested, I know a great club called Hill Huggers. It's Whittington's best organized off-road club. Give them a try if you want to do any more four-wheeling. I think they have a meet scheduled this weekend."

It was late afternoon and Adam was congratulating himself on having followed the red-haired man to his apartment earlier in the week. Listening to the CD he'd taken from the woman's house confirmed it wasn't *The Sound of Music* arrangement containing the Alliance's plans. It might be that the CD he was looking for had been taken by the red-haired man.

Today Adam's truck had a magnetic sign that said PIZZA. It also had a pizza oven that was currently warming a tomato pizza. He parked and carried the warm pizza with him when he climbed the stairs to knock on the red-haired man's apartment door. When no one answered, Adam picked the cheap lock and entered, putting the pizza on the kitchen table while he looked around. Almost immediately he spotted a collection of CDs lining three shelves of a bookcase. He hurried over and began searching, dragging his finger slowly along the rows as he read titles. When he came to *The Sound of Music*, he pulled it from the shelf, only to discover it wasn't the version he needed. He checked the other CDs, but the arrangement he was looking for wasn't there. Grabbing the pizza, he hurried back to his truck and headed for the woman's house. He would return her copy of *The Sound of Music*, and search more carefully for the copy he needed.

CHAPTER
15

Shortly after five, Connor returned home. He hurried to the refrigerator for a cold beer and drank half of it with the refrigerator door still open. It had been a hard week trying to keep his by-line on page one. Unfortunately a death at the Stettler pre-empted his fifth page-one story. He settled on the sofa and tried to decide where his Sam Morgan story could go next.

As he drank the last of the beer, it occurred to him that he was starved for pizza. He sniffed several times, realizing he'd smelled pizza the moment he stepped into his apartment. Of course that didn't make sense; he hadn't brought pizza home in over a week. Had he forgotten to take the garbage out? He checked. No, it was empty.

Still, the hint of spicy tomato sauce lingered in the air. He checked his oven. No pizza. A startling idea occurred and he walked slowly through the apartment, searching for something to confirm a growing suspicion. And then he glanced at his music collection.

He always put his favorite jazz recording on the shelf with its leading edge poking out from the others. That trick enabled him to lay his hands on it quickly. But today it was lined up with all the others. Connor's breath caught in his throat. Someone *had* been in his apartment and they'd messed with his music collection. He stared at the line-up. What else had they messed with?

###

"It smells like pizza, all right," Tom agreed as he and Teddy entered her house. "I don't suppose you've been indulging in midnight snacks that didn't include me?"

"You and I had pizza for lunch yesterday, but we disposed of the box as we left, and the leftovers are still in the refrigerator."

"But your house smells like fresh pizza."

"Oh, oh!" Teddy pointed at her desktop where a CD case rested on a letter she'd been writing the previous evening. "I didn't put that recording there." She reached for it.

"Hold it." Tom grabbed her arm to pull her away, then holding her close, whispered in her ear, "If you didn't put it there, is it a CD you're familiar with? Is it yours?"

"Probably," she whispered back.

"Explain. I'll sweep for bugs in a minute."

"It's a recording of *The Sound of Music*. I have two copies now that Frances Ravensworth gave me a second one. I left my old copy on the desk, intending to give it away. What I didn't do was put it on the letter I wrote last night."

"Okay," Tom whispered. "About the second copy, did Frances hand it to you?" He shifted his weight restlessly, becoming painfully aware of Teddy's sensuous body close to his. The sweet fragrance of her hair filled his nostrils.

"No. She slipped it in my tote just as she's done other times. She likes to surprise me."

"Where is the second copy?" Tom whispered, his lips brushing the side of her face as he spoke.

"In my car stereo. I meant to play it when I drove to work this morning, but I had too much on my mind."

"Where's your car now?"

"You drove me home, so it's still in the parking lot a block from the Stettler."

Tom planted a light kiss on Teddy's forehead, and hurried to the front door. "I'll be right back." He punched numbers on his cell phone as he rushed from the house. Standing just beyond her front door in case the house was bugged, he reached a number available to only a few people. He gave instructions, then returned to Teddy's living room to sweep it. Hopefully the agents searching her car would find the CD that duplicated her copy, and it would contain the information everyone had been searching for.

###

"I tell you," grumped Lydia Plummer, "the neighborly thing to do is let Teddy know her repairman is upsetting Bullet. If we don't, those grouchy neighbors across the street will call the cops again." Lydia reached out to stroke a black and brown German shepherd as she argued with her bed-ridden spouse.

"Teddy will think we're *nosey Parkers*," Burt Plummer replied, pushing a button to adjust his bed.

"*Neighborhood Watch*! That's what the sign on the street says. It's what people who stay home do for those who have to go to work."

"Okay. Don't bother listening to me." Burt heaved his bulk from his bed into a wheelchair. "Go ahead and do what you want, just like you always do." He pressed a button, launching the chair toward the kitchen where dinner waited.

"Well, thanks for your support," Lydia replied sarcastically. She let the door bang behind her as she left the house. It wouldn't do to give Burt too much information, but at the moment there was a downright handsome man in Teddy Sanderson's house. Lydia Plummer intended to find out more about him and more about Teddy's other men.

###

As Tom completed the second sweep of Teddy's house, the doorbell rang. Teddy stepped to the door. "Just a minute," she called, looking through the peephole. Behind her Tom ditched his equipment.

The elderly woman on the front porch shouted, "I need to talk to you."

"It's my neighbor," Teddy whispered, making sure Tom's equipment was out of sight. She opened the door. "Hi, Lydia. What can I do for you?"

"You can invite me in, out of the cold. I have some complaints I want to get off my chest."

"Invite the lady in," called Tom from the sofa.

Lydia pushed her way past Teddy and headed for Tom. "I'm Lydia Plummer, Teddy's neighbor to the west." Lydia pointed at one of Teddy's walls to indicate the direction. "And you?" The question dangled invitingly as she extended her hand to be shaken.

Special Agent Heeter stood and smiled as he shook hands with Lydia. "I'm Tom, Teddy's boyfriend," he said.

"*Niiiice* going, Teddy," the diminutive neighbor said. She gave Teddy a sly smile. "This one might be a keeper."

Teddy flushed. "You said you had complaints. I'm not home enough to be a bad neighbor, am I?"

"It's not you I'm complaining about. It's that repairman of yours—the one who keeps showing up and ignoring Bullet so he barks and wakes Burt." She turned toward Tom and explained, "My husband is crippled and has trouble resting, so any sleep he gets, day or night, is a blessing to both of us."

Tom looked at Teddy, noting her puzzled expression. "Miss Lydia," he said, "are you sure it's really a repairman or does my girl have another honey she's not telling me about?"

Lydia straightened up. "Burt and I assumed the guy was a repairman. He showed up the first time in a white van with writing on the side. Today he came with a pizza. It looked like he let himself in with the key from under her mat."

"A repairman who brings his own lunch along? I could use someone like him to work on my apartment," Tom said. "Do you know which company sent him?"

"I can't remember the name on his truck, but it had a cute slogan. *We Light Up Your Life.* Something easy to remember."

"Sounds like an electrician. That should help me find him," Tom said. "Are you sure it was the same man who brought pizza today?"

"Absolutely. Same exact fellow with short, jet-black curls. Today he didn't go around to Teddy's back door like he did last time. He just walked right in through the front door, bold as anything." She shook her finger at Teddy. "You should know better than to leave a door unlocked or hand out keys."

"You're right, Lydia," Teddy said. "I need to be more careful." The puzzled look was still on Teddy's face when the ringing phone interrupted. "Hello," she said, nodding as she listened. "She's standing right here. I'll tell her you want her home immediately."

"Can't be out of Burt's sight more than two minutes," grumped Lydia, heading for the door. "You will tell that guy to talk to Bullet, won't you? All Bullet wants is to be acknowledged. It's people who ignore him that get him riled up."

"One more question, Lydia," Tom said. "Do you have anything to add to the description of Teddy's repairman except for black hair? I should find out what my competition looks like." He smiled.

"Easy," Lydia replied, returning Tom's smile. "The guy wasn't to my taste since he had a big beak." She thumped her nose in case Tom didn't understand. "He wasn't very tall and didn't weigh a whole lot. It's all that black, curly hair that sets him apart."

"Okay, I'll make an appointment to dye my hair and curl it. Thanks for the tip, Lydia."

The giggling neighbor paused to take one last look at Tom. She leaned toward Teddy and whispered, "You ought to encourage him to go ahead with the dye job and the perm. That would at least give him the look of that other guy you've got nosing around."

"Whoa!" Tom jumped from the sofa to stop Lydia. He put one arm around Teddy's waist. "What other guy? Teddy has another boyfriend?" He pulled Teddy close.

Lydia nodded. "He talks to Bullet so he isn't a problem. Teddy knows who I'm talking about." Lydia pointed at a picture on the wall next to the front door. The picture was a candid shot of Gene and Frances taken years earlier. They had attended a silent auction and Frances had bid successfully on a puzzle package. Teddy captured the moment her best friend opened it and realized the package contained a marriage proposal from Gene Ravensworth. The expression on Frances's face was one Teddy treasured.

"That man doesn't have black hair," Tom said, resting a finger on Gene Ravensworth.

"Not him," Lydia said. "That guy in the background." She pointed to an indistinct figure behind Gene and Frances. "You better pay attention," Lydia said. "I'm telling you, Teddy likes men with dark, curly hair." She gave Tom a knowing wink and headed out the door.

Tom turned back to Teddy. She had turned pale and her hands were shaking.

"My God!" she whispered, pointing with a trembling finger. "Lydia means Myron. If Myron's been here, I need to look for booby-traps."

CHAPTER
16

Teddy's inquisitive neighbor, Lydia Plummer, hurried into her house just as Connor parked across the street. He noticed the woman leaving Teddy's, but when she didn't get in the Camry sitting in Teddy's driveway, he became curious. Who did the Camry belong to?

That's what I need, a mysterious someone in my story. Connor smiled. He set the brake and hurried to Teddy's front porch. Ignoring the bell, he raised his hand to thump her door.

###

"More company?" Tom asked, having just settled on the sofa.

"It's Connor," Teddy said. "I saw him parking across the street as Lydia left. Were you present during his interviews?"

Tom shook his head. "I didn't even pass him in the hallway."

"Okay, then here we go." Teddy opened the door before Connor could bang on it again. "Connor!" she exclaimed.

"Have I come at a bad time?"

"Not at all. Come in and meet my friend from high school." She turned toward the FBI agent. "Tom, this is Connor Douglas. He's the man who helped me when Mr. Morgan collapsed."

The two men nodded and shook hands. "I was driving past your neighborhood just now," Connor said. "I thought, you know, that you might have heard something new; something that might...." His voice trailed off.

Teddy gestured toward a chair and watched him sink into it. "As far as I know, nothing new has turned up. How about you? Any success talking with Bradford?"

"Only briefly. He promised to leave you out of his stories." Connor looked first at Tom and then at Teddy. "Crap," he said. "The real reason I stopped was to tell you someone broke into my apartment." He pulled his cap from his coat pocket and began nervously twisting it.

Tom and Teddy stared at him. "What makes you think someone broke in?" Tom asked.

"When I came home," Connor began, "I didn't notice anything strange at first. Then it dawned on me the apartment smelled like pizza." He looked at Tom and then at Teddy. "I haven't had pizza in a week. There's no way that smell should be in my apartment unless someone entered it with a pizza." He looked at his audience again. "What I'm saying sounds crazy, doesn't it?"

Teddy and Tom glanced at each other. Not only had there been the hint of spicy pizza at Teddy's when they entered, but Lydia Plummer had just told them about a man entering Teddy's house carrying one.

"I didn't imagine it!" Connor insisted, looking from one person to the other.

"Is there anything else that makes you think someone was in your apartment?" Tom asked.

Connor hesitated. "I'm particular with how I arrange my music collection. My CDs had been messed with."

"That *is* interesting," Tom said. "Were any taken?"

"I didn't check. It gave me the creeps to think someone had been handling my stuff. I got out of there as fast as I could."

"I'm not sure it makes sense that a burglar broke in carrying his lunch," Tom said.

Connor nodded. "I know."

"How about pizza remains? Leftovers? A box in your garbage?"

"None of those. I did check on that. There was nothing; only the smell of pizza." He looked at Tom, and then at Teddy.

Teddy said, "Could your visitor have been a friend playing a joke?"

"They'd have to jimmy my lock." Connor's voice slid up the scale, then he paused. "Hey, do you think...?" He directed the question at Teddy. "Do you think it could be, you know, the guys who took Morgan out?"

Teddy said, "That would make sense. Maybe they think you've got whatever Sam Morgan took from them. They didn't find it in my house or office." She turned to Tom. "What do you think, Tom?"

"I think Connor should be extra careful and get some new security installed." He turned to the nervous young man. "I assume, like Teddy, you've been interviewed by the FBI. You should call whoever you talked to there and bring that person up-to-date. They might want to dust for prints."

Connor gulped. "You sound like a cop. What is it you do?"

"I'm between jobs," Tom replied.

"That doesn't answer my question," Connor said.

"Okay, I'll be more specific. I have a law degree, but I don't want to be a lawyer. Like I said, I'm between jobs at the moment."

Disappointment showed on Connor's face. He turned back to Teddy. "How could Sam's murderer find me? Bradford hasn't mentioned me in his columns."

"We know I'm being watched," Teddy said, "and you've visited me here and at the office."

"You think they followed me? Is that what you're suggesting?" Connor's eyes opened wide.

Teddy nodded. "They know you and I helped Sam, so...." She let the thought dangle.

"I think I'll leave town for a while. I have a friend I can stay with." Connor twisted his car keys now that his cap was on his head. "I think I'll go there for the weekend."

"Good idea," Tom agreed.

Connor hurried to the door, slamming it as he left.

Teddy looked at Tom. "What's your take on this evening's events? If the pizza man was at Connor's and here too, then this place must have been searched again."

"I'm not surprised Connor's getting visits. That pretty much tells us that whatever Sam got away with hasn't been recovered. Whoever the recipient should have been is serious about wanting it back. They're looking at every person and every angle they can think of."

Tom's intensity made Teddy uncomfortable. She said, "If they didn't hesitate to kill an FBI agent, they certainly won't hesitate to kill me or Connor. Or even you if you get in the way."

"That brings us to the next subject needing discussion. First of all, I've meant to compliment you on the new hair style. It's very attractive. Next, tell me about any plans you had for this weekend—before your world started falling apart."

"I nearly forgot." Teddy jumped to her feet, grabbing her day planner from the desk. "Frances invited me to dinner tomorrow to celebrate my first week as a professional Girl Friday." She paused, "I also planned to visit an off-road club for a couple of hours on Sunday."

"You don't look like the four-wheeling type," Tom said.

"I'm not. I'm hunting for a blue truck with a special mount on the front bumper. I think the driver tried to kill a friend of mine."

"I see. Unfortunately your unstructured time is when you're most vulnerable to attack, and since Connor's been including your personal information in his stories, you're easy to find. I suspect this weekend will include a vigorous attempt to retrieve whatever Sam had."

"Are you suggesting his killers will show up here?"

Tom shrugged. "They have two days before anyone misses you or expects to see you at work. Because home is where you are expected to be alone and have your guard down, I think it's a safe bet they'll make an attempt of some kind."

"What should I do?" Worry lines etched Teddy's face.

"I suggest you get ready to spend the weekend at the apartment on Canyon Street."

She stared at him. "If I move to your apartment where will you be?"

"It's this way, *girlfriend*." He emphasized the word to remind her of the role he'd been assigned to play in her life. "I'd appreciate it if you didn't spoil my reputation as a lady killer by advertising the fact that I'll be in the second bedroom. Alone." He smiled. "Now grab your suitcase and let's go."

Teddy reached for the telephone instead. "First I'll give Frances a call and see if I can either get you invited to dinner tomorrow, or get my invitation rescheduled."

###

Teddy's first night in the Canyon Street apartment went relatively well. Tom spent the evening studying something he didn't share with her, and she tried unsuccessfully to get interested in a mystery novel that didn't hold a candle to her real life. Her only productive work was a call to Gene Ravensworth to ask for a legal aid contact so she could check Thelma Rasmussen's work experience and her abilities. If the woman checked out, she'd be hired.

The next morning, when the phone rang, Tom answered it. After almost no conversation on his part, he hung up, and turned to Teddy. "I need you to promise you won't leave this apartment. I'm needed in Brighton's office, but I'll return in time for dinner with the Ravensworths." Teddy gave her word, and Tom took off, pushing the speed limit all the way to the Stettler Building.

###

"Before we start," Dillard began, "I've put in a call to Gwen Morgan about her newest parolee, Myron Ratini. She meets with him this afternoon to check on his progress. If he's messed up the terms of his release and we can prove it, he'll end up back in prison and no longer be a worry to Sanderson."

"That would help," Tom said. "She's genuinely afraid of the guy." He reached for the coffee cup Dillard offered. "We know he's screwed up because he called while I was there and Teddy's neighbor has seen him skulking around Teddy's place."

"That's probably not good enough without film to back it up. Anyway, Gwen said she'd be in touch later today after she sees him. As I recall, Sanderson wasn't happy with the prospect of you camping out with her. How's it going now?"

"We've worked out a system, so we're getting along pretty well."

"That's good. Now then, let's get down to business." Dillard held up a CD. "Here's what everyone's been looking for."

The disk appeared to be a recording of *The Sound of Music*, and nothing more. Tom said, "They must have encrypted the important stuff."

Dillard nodded. "Unless one knew to look for the information hidden here, they'd never suspect it existed. We had to involve our most knowledgeable experts to decode the encryptions."

Dillard slid the CD into an unfamiliar machine. A moment later his hands flew over the keyboard. Graphics with what looked like pages of sophisticated codes, showed up. The men studied the data. "Whoever encrypted this material is a competent, organized hacker," Dillard said. "We don't know the country of origin, but we know that with the help of a certain element in this country, this information will enable cybercriminals to cause big problems. To protect critical infrastructure from cyber-attacks, we have to work with both device manufacturers and system operators to reduce the risks and costs of those attacks. The latest in specialized hardware needs to be installed before members of the Delphi Alliance get their hands on information like this.

"As fast as new defensive mechanisms are invented, the attackers will develop their own more sophisticated programs. Most hackers aren't prepared to deal with the reality of a control system, but a small subset is prepared to dig into control systems and take over their operation. We can only guess at the intent of the Alliance. We don't know if they want to take over systems or just interfere with their ability to perform as they should."

Dillard sighed. "We'll need to alert various agencies, and get them involved. It may be that whoever prepared this information isn't local, but resides outside the States." Dillard pushed his hair back. "They may suspect we have their plans, but of equal importance is Sanderson's ability to ID the man she observed when Sam died." He studied Tom's face. "You need to keep a close eye on her. Keep checking for listening devices in her car, her home, and even in her office. The advantage is ours, but only for the moment. As soon as the information can be duplicated, the Alliance won't need this copy. When that happens, they may consider getting rid of Sanderson and Douglas."

Tom studied his friend before leaning back in his chair. "She's the surest link we have to catching Sam's killer or to breaking up this organization."

Dillard nodded. "She's the only one who can identify the man who searched Sam or the one who installed listening devices in her office. If we don't include her in our operation, we could lose her trust."

Tom frowned.

"All we have at the moment," Dillard continued, "is an on-going collection of subjects who need to be identified and neutralized."

"Now that we know the Alliance's plans, we can contact agencies and alert them to beef up their infrastructure." Tom looked up. "Connor Douglas had his apartment broken into yesterday. How about using him? If we…."

"Hold that thought." Dillard reached for the intercom on his desk. "Helen, continue holding my calls for the time being, but bring me the file on Connor Douglas." He turned back to Tom. "Okay. Let's hear your plan."

###

Gwen Morgan sat opposite Myron Ratini. "How's it going, Myron?" she asked. "Have you found a job yet?"

Myron's hands moved nervously as they picked at imaginary lint on his dark slacks. "Not yet. My prison record makes good jobs hard to come by, but I've got goals and I'm working toward them." Myron tried not to laugh as he met Gwen's questioning eyes. His goals were to kill Teddy Sanderson and get out of the country.

"Where have you applied?" Gwen asked.

"I've pretty much checked out the good job openings listed in the newspaper and on-line."

"And?"

"And I'm not going to take a dish washing job or learn to flip burgers in some snot-nosed fast-food joint. Those jobs are for teenagers and senior citizens."

"Sometimes that's where you have to work to pay your bills. Sometimes it's where you need to work as you wait for the perfect job to open up." Gwen picked up her pen and made a few notes in Myron's file. "Have you stayed away from your former wife? No calls? No drive-by?" Her pen rested above the forms.

Myron watched her suspiciously. He didn't want her recording things that could put him back in prison. He needed to move ahead quickly with his plans for his ex-wife. "This town isn't all that big," he complained. "I thought I saw her when I was getting my car serviced, but I couldn't be sure." His eyes shifted away from the parole officer's gaze. "I've been watching my step. I haven't gone out of my way to look her up."

"You do understand, don't you, that if, as you say, this small town throws you two together, you're the one who has to move out of the area."

"Yeah, I know. The parole board made that clear. I'm not stupid enough to do something that'll put me back in the slammer." He crossed his legs, jiggling one foot nervously up and down.

Gwen shuffled papers in his file and added some notes. "I want to see you back here at this same time next week."

"Another Saturday?"

"I'm getting ready to take some time off. When you come next week you need to have a job, or a list of interviews you've been on or have lined up. Do you understand?"

Myron got to his feet. "Sure. I'll see you at this same time next week, with a list." A satisfied smile crossed his face. The parole officer had just established the exact moment when Teddy Sanderson Ratini would die. It was a deadline he was eager to keep.

CHAPTER

17

As Teddy and Tom walked toward the Ravensworth's front door that evening Tom said, "Clue me in on Ravensworth's wife. He's an attorney. Is she employed?"

"Frances considers herself a housewife with a hobby. She designs and creates costumes for theater productions."

"That should give us something interesting to discuss," Tom said, pushing the doorbell a second time.

"Come in, come in," invited Gene Ravensworth, grinning. He stepped back to let his guests enter.

Teddy said, "Gene, this is my friend, Tom Heeter." She turned toward Tom. "Gene is a former employer who had the good sense to marry my best friend."

The men nodded as they shook hands. Gene said, "Frances is in the kitchen, but she'll join us in a minute."

At that moment Frances entered the room. "I thought I heard the doorbell," she said, greeting her guests. Teddy helped get things ready and before long they were seated around the dining room table.

"Tom was telling me," Gene began, turning to his wife, "that he went to high school with Teddy."

"What? You went to Franklin High School in Portland?" Frances looked stunned.

"That's right," Tom said, gazing fondly at Teddy. "That's where we met."

"What years were you there?" Frances asked. "Did you graduate from Franklin?"

Tom shook his head. "I only attended my freshman year," he said. "My family moved out of the district after that."

"Were you in any of Teddy's classes?"

"I think we had basic English and math together," Tom said with confidence; all students took those classes. He looked at Teddy and was reassured when she returned his smile.

"Then you had old fuddy duddy Dawson! What a circus that class turned out to be." Frances laughed.

"Calling him a fuddy duddy is going a little far, don't you think?" Tom grinned back at Frances.

"Her," Teddy corrected quickly, looking at the startled face of the friend she'd gone to grade school and high school with. "You've gotten Mrs. Dawson mixed up with some other teacher."

Frances was looking at Tom through narrowed eyes.

"It was all so long ago," Tom said, laughing. "After my family moved there were so many other teachers."

Frances continued watching her dinner guest suspiciously. "I didn't think anyone could forget Dawson."

Gene looked aghast at his usually polite wife. Then he saw the expression on Tom Heeter's face. "What gives?" Gene asked.

Teddy interrupted, "Tom, I forgot to tell you that Frances was at Franklin, too."

"I see," he said.

"Teddy? Is there something you aren't telling us?" Frances turned her suspicious look on her friend.

Teddy shrugged her shoulders, watching Tom reach into his pocket.

"It looks like my roommate and I didn't prepare adequately for your third degree, Frances," Tom said, flashing his FBI identification. "When we get back to *our* apartment tonight we'll have something to chat about, won't we, Teddy, dear?"

Frances had a startled look on her face.

Gene laughed. "Drop it, Frances. No more questions. Just pass the wine to Tom. I think he could use a refresher."

When dinner was over Teddy and Tom waved their farewells and walked to Tom's gray Camry. "I'm sorry about that slip-up," Teddy said. "It didn't occur to me that Frances would ask such detailed questions."

Tom shook his head and gave a sideways glance at the woman beside him as he opened the car door for her. For once she seemed totally relaxed and that pleased him. He got in the car, checked his rear view mirror, and headed to Canyon Street.

Teddy said, "It felt good to let my worries melt away tonight. Life has been scary lately, and you did look delightfully helpless fumbling your way through Frances's version of a third degree." She watched Tom negotiate a busy intersection, suddenly aware they'd traveled through it moments earlier. "We're retracing our route. Are we being followed?" She sat up straight, turning to examine the traffic behind them.

"There's no one interested in us at the moment, but it never hurts to make sure." Tom made a sharp left turn followed quickly by two more lefts. "We're looking good," he said. A few minutes later he parked in front of the Canyon Street apartment house.

Teddy shivered. The brief respite was over. Real life was back. She stood quietly as Tom unlocked the door to the apartment. The reason she'd been paired with this attractive man was clear once more. It was a reality that grabbed at her stomach, bringing thoughts of her murderous ex-husband back to life. "You said you'd talk to Brighton about the conditions for Myron's parole. Is there anything new I should know?"

"Not at the moment." Tom walked into the apartment, flipping on lights. "Dillard talked to Myron's parole officer and she planned to meet with him this afternoon. She'll check to see if he's resisting his impulses to bug you." He helped Teddy off with her coat, and swung his jacket over a chair.

"We already know he hasn't resisted. You listened in when he phoned and Lydia Plummer saw him at my house." Teddy frowned.

"I told Dillard about those episodes. I'm sure he's passed that information on to Gwen." Tom plopped into a comfortable chair.

"Myron isn't going to find a job. He doesn't want one. The only job he ever held was when he worked for his Uncle Vinnie, before Vinnie cleaned up his act." The look on Teddy's face was sober. She settled stiffly on the sofa.

"Myron is Vinnie Ratini's nephew?"

Teddy nodded.

"I wonder if Dillard's aware of *that*? We need to check out the players in our drama, and learn about their loyalties. How did you get along with the uncle?"

"Fine. He liked me then and I have no reason to believe anything's changed."

"Are you sure?"

She nodded "It was Uncle Vinnie who made my leaving Myron so easy."

"Where is Uncle Vinnie now?"

"Probably in Arizona. Maybe Hawaii. Sometimes he goes to Italy where he grew up." She pulled off her shoes and curled her legs beneath her, sinking back in the sofa cushions.

"If you needed to call on him for help, would he come to your aid?"

"I think so," she responded. "I can't imagine anything has changed our relationship." When Tom didn't comment, Teddy glanced at him.

"Time has a way of changing things," he said.

###

The next day, while Teddy made lists of agencies where she could send her *open for business* announcements, Tom consulted with a friend about a truck he wanted to borrow.

"Are you sure you can handle a rig like this?" Eric asked Tom, one arm protectively resting on his vehicle with its twenty-inch wheels and five-inch lift. "Off-road you need to know how to handle all types of terrain and conditions."

"Your truck is certainly a big one," Tom said, studying the massive vehicle. "I haven't done much driving over rugged terrain."

"Who're you going with?" Eric asked, polishing an invisible spot of dust on the driver's door.

"Hill Huggers. We leave High Cliffs at eleven."

"I know that area. It takes you over fairly rugged country with narrow, graveled roads. Some of them are pretty steep." Eric looked at his friend, his forehead covered with worry lines. "Would you object to me tagging along? Driving the rig myself?"

"Sure! Why not? Teddy and I were planning to head out at ten. She thinks a member of Hill Huggers is a hit-and-run driver in a case she's helping with."

"Have you got emergency supplies?"

"Like what?"

"That settles it," Eric replied laughing. "I'm not letting you head off-road alone. Dillard would demote me to a desk job. I'll get some things together and pick you two up on Canyon Street at ten."

The caravan of two small Suzuki Samurai leading a group of three all-terrain vehicles and five four-wheelers slowly made its way up a narrow cut in the hill they'd been climbing for two hours. As one ATV scooted past Eric's rig, he slowed to make sure he could squeeze past an ugly outcropping of granite.

"You think we'll get past without scratching your truck?" Teddy asked.

"Clear on my side," Eric responded.

"Clear over here," Tom echoed as Eric negotiated the pass and drove into the clearing where drivers and passengers expected to eat lunch.

"It's about time!" The greeting came from a man lounging in a lawn chair near a campfire. "Lunch was ready half an hour ago." He pushed himself from the lawn chair and edged toward a table where he began stirring the stew he'd been cooking.

"Hey, Wendell," one of the ATV drivers called. "We got us some first timers."

"Not all of us are newbies," grumbled Eric under his breath.

"How can I help?" Teddy asked.

"Take this to the table and help set things up." Eric handed her a picnic basket and cooler. "Tom and I need to check my rig for debris that might be lodged in the undercarriage." The men walked back to Eric's truck, while Teddy cautiously approached the tables.

"What'a ya got?" Wendell asked her, reaching out for the cooler.

"I'm not sure," she replied, beginning to unpack sandwiches and condiments from the picnic basket as she studied the beefy man whose dark hair formed the unruly beard resting on his chest.

"Cold things go to the other end of the table," Wendell instructed. "When you get done with that, you could pull the beer out of the cab of my truck and bring it over. Do it quietly. My old lady's sleeping in the camper." He nodded in the direction of a blue truck with a detachable camper.

"Wow!" exclaimed Teddy. "That's a mean looking rig, you've got." She was looking at the vehicle's front bumper with its extra steel plates and upright supports reinforced with "D" ring mounts. She carried beer back to Wendell. "Is that what Eric refers to as a bull bar?"

"You got it. Now see if you can help Gramps take food back to his truck. He's too stiff to sit on blankets with the rest of us."

The eighty-year-old member of the Hill Huggers nodded at Teddy and indicated what she could carry for him, then he slowly moved toward the truck he'd been riding in.

"Wendell looks like he's been camping, doesn't he?" Teddy said, making conversation as she and Gramps walked toward his rig.

"Wendell Green's a lucky man! Able to camp out from time to time. Makes me wish I was young again." Gramps climbed into the cab of his truck and reached for the food Teddy was carrying.

"How's it going?" Tom asked, joining her as she helped get the old man settled.

"Except for a couple of small problems, it's going well." She handed a bottle of soda to Gramps, before joining Tom and whispering, "Wendell's *old lady* is asleep in his truck—the one with the bull bar on the front bumper. If his old lady is Sally Anne Smith, she'll recognize me as Ella Jones. The problem is, I paid the required fees with a card using my real name."

Tom gave a quiet whistle. "I think you have a headache coming on. Wrap a scarf around your head and put on sunglasses. Get back in Eric's truck. I'll bring you something to eat and let him know it's time to head back. What's the other problem?"

"Dillard told me my anonymous phone threat was made by Wendell Green. That's the name of the man dishing stew."

"Then the threat was aimed at your involvement with the Smith divorce instead of Sam's death or the Alliance. I wonder if Wendell is a member of the Alliance?"

Teddy shrugged her shoulders and hurried to Eric's truck. She covered her face as much as possible. As they prepared to leave, Sally Anne showed up at the lunch table and began filling her plate. Teddy took snapshots of Sally Anne talking to Wendell. She felt sure William Smith's hit-and-run driver would soon be answering questions after William's attorney saw Teddy's pictures and gave copies to the police.

CHAPTER
18

Myron was making plans. It was time to get serious about Teddy. For a price he could pick up a driver's license, a passport and a gun. The gun would be for Adam to use on Teddy, and the fake ID would take Myron to the Cayman Islands where his pre-prison, laundered money waited. If he arranged for the ID today, he'd have it by the end of the week.

He'd keep his Saturday appointment with the parole officer while Adam made use of the gun. When his appointment with Gwen Morgan ended he'd have the perfect alibi for the time of Teddy's death. He'd leave Gwen's office an innocent man, and disappear into a new life. It was perfect.

The parolee whistled a happy tune. Life was good.

###

Teddy was relieved to get home early Monday morning. She quickly changed clothes, and then hurried to the office to prepare for the arrival of the woman she'd hired to assist with office tasks.

Her new employee, Thelma Rasmussen, arrived promptly at eight, and got busy addressing the envelopes Teddy had waiting for her.

Teddy sorted various reports the attorneys wanted, made a series of phone calls, and then settled back to read the *News Telegrapher*. Connor's article for the day had a headline that read: "FBI inquiry targets First Amendment." It featured the Delphi Alliance's left-wing activities operating under federal scrutiny, and was a vague rehash of old reports and editorials. For Connor it was new territory. He was a crime reporter and usually stayed away from politics.

"I've finished addressing the envelopes," Thelma said, interrupting Teddy. "And I have the addresses entered in a computer file."

"Good job. Why don't you go for an early lunch," Teddy suggested. "I'll see you again at one."

"Thanks. I'd like that." Thelma grabbed her coat and hurried out the door.

Teddy finished organizing reports as the office door suddenly opened.

"Don't you stop for lunch?" Tom asked, stepping into the room. "Grab your coat and let's find something to eat."

Teddy pushed away from her desk. "You don't have to ask me twice," she said.

At a deli nearby, Teddy and Tom settled down with Caesar salads. "To what do I owe this treat?" she asked.

"Brighton wants you to know that the drop Sam intercepted has been recovered by our department."

"Perfect," Teddy breathed. "Then all this breaking into my home and office will end."

"That probably won't happen."

"Why not?" She put her fork down and stared at Tom.

"Because what I've just told you is privileged information. We aren't telling anyone else."

"Do you mean the bad guys will still be looking for it?"

"I'm afraid so." He studied her worried face. "And then there's Dillard's request."

Teddy frowned and picked through her salad, glancing at Tom's serious expression. "I already know I'm not going to like whatever it is."

"He wants you to give Thelma her own key to your office."

"I don't want to do that."

"He wants her to feel trusted and at ease."

"Are you suggesting that she's one of the bad guys?"

Tom didn't answer that question. "He's hoping it will help bring this case to a close. If that happens, you won't have me as a roommate any more. That should appeal to you."

"You drive a hard bargain," Teddy said with a smile.

###

When five o'clock arrived, Teddy handed Thelma an office key. "I only have two of these, so be careful not to lose this one."

"I'll be very careful," Thelma said.

They bid each other good night and Teddy drove home alone, to be joined later by Tom.

As she set the table, she glanced at the time. Seven o'clock. She froze, staring at the timepiece. Something about it bothered her. There was something about that hour she was supposed to remember.

And then it surfaced.

She'd promised to make a call to England in the morning to accommodate the nine-hour time difference. The telephone numbers and the case numbers she needed were at the office. Teddy sighed, and after grabbing her coat, she headed back to the Stettler.

###

At the Stettler, lights burned in various office windows. Teddy reluctantly pulled into her usual basement parking slot and hurried across the deserted space, her footsteps echoing in the darkness. The dimly lit area felt ominous at night and she couldn't help looking over her shoulder as she pushed a button and listened for the elevator as it clanked down to the lowest level. The doors opened and she stepped in.

She was grateful for the warmth of the small space and the comforting whir as the elevator rose to the fourth floor. Walking toward her office, she was jolted by the silence of the place and the lack of hall lights, even though the burned out bulb near her office had been replaced.

There was no sign of the custodial staff, a testament to their having finished work on this floor. At her office door Teddy searched for her key, and then paused. A ribbon of light shown through the door's frosted glass. Had the cleaning staff forgotten to turn off the lights or had her burglar returned?

Heart pounding, Teddy quietly inserted her key in the lock and listened to the deadbolt give a small tick. Slowly she turned the door knob, and in a rush, flung the door open.

The figure going through her desk drawers looked up, startled by the interruption.

"What the hell do you think you're doing?" Teddy demanded of her new secretary. "Get away from my desk."

"Th-thank goodness you came back," stammered Thelma. "I was looking for your home phone number. You didn't give it to me." Thelma closed the drawer she'd been pawing through. "I need to let you know I can't come to work in the morning. One of the twins came home from school tonight with chickenpox."

"My number is listed in the phone book, Thelma."

Thelma's eyes changed from friendly confusion to something more calculating. She took a step toward Teddy. "I guess I didn't think of a solution as simple as looking in the phone book." Her voice was low. She took another step forward. "Now that I've given you my news, I'll go home and tend to the boys." The look on Thelma's face made Teddy shiver.

"Stop right where you are," Teddy said, taking a step backward, away from Thelma. Her breath caught in her throat, and she froze. In front of her was a woman who looked like she could kill, and behind her was a firm body blocking any escape.

"What's taking you so long?" asked the voice Teddy was coming to recognize and rely on. She jerked her head around and saw Tom looking down at her. He wasn't smiling.

Thelma had paused.

"Tom," Teddy whispered, sinking into the warmth of arms that tightened around her.

"You ladies shouldn't work all day *and* all night," he chided. "You need to take time off for beauty sleep. Is this your new secretary, Teddy? Aren't you going to introduce us?"

"I'm Thelma Rasmussen," the secretary offered in a rush. "Teddy didn't ask me to work late. I came back on my own to look for her home phone number. One of my twins has the chickenpox, and I was so upset that it didn't occur to me Teddy would be listed in the phone book."

"Isn't chickenpox contagious?" Tom asked. "You'll be tied up nursing kids for days."

Thelma nodded. "I can imagine what this must have looked like to Teddy when she opened the door and found me rummaging through her desk drawers." Thelma's short laugh sounded forced.

Teddy extended her hand. "Why don't I take your key back for now? As I said earlier, I only have two of them and I may need to get someone else in to help out during your absence."

Thelma handed her key to Teddy. "I'll call once Cole is well and is able to return to school."

Teddy nodded and moved to her file cabinet. "I forgot to take the Sebring file when I left."

Thelma said, "It's time I got back to tending to my sick kid." She eased past Tom and headed down the hall.

"Oh, Tom," Teddy sighed, ready to pour out the fear she'd felt.

He placed his index finger against her lips to remind her of the listening devices, then took her gently into his arms, and held her close.

"I'll drive you home," he whispered against her soft hair. He knew the listening device installed by Dillard would let his boss know that he wouldn't be back tonight. Tom was glad his department had installed their own *ears* in Teddy's office. There was no telling what Thelma Rasmussen might have done if he hadn't shown up.

Having received Tom's message that he'd drive Teddy home instead of returning to the office, Dillard set aside the documents he and Tom had been studying. He rose from his chair, stretched the kinks from his tired muscles, and punched a button to leave a message for his secretary. He wanted the file on Thelma Rasmussen, along with files on anyone else at her address or that she might be related to. He knew that in the morning Tom would ask about the new secretary, and the degree of danger she posed to Teddy. Dillard wanted to have answers readily available.

"What do you mean she caught you going through her desk?" Raz looked at his wife as she threw her coat over a chair.

"Just what I said. We left for the day, but I went back after a couple of hours to make a more thorough search of her office than what Isaac's agent did. While I was there she came back to get a file she forgot to take home." Thelma sat opposite her husband and unfolded the employment form she'd stolen from Teddy's files. Slowly she began shredding it.

"And did she really forget a file, or was that a ruse to explain why she returned? Maybe you did something foolish and she was suspicious of you."

Thelma said, "I know she planned to take the file home. It has something to do with an English citizen. Because of the time difference she was supposed to call authorities the minute she wakes up in the morning." Thelma leaned back in the chair, closing her eyes.

"What about your chickenpox story, do you think she bought it?" He put his newspaper aside.

"She believed the one about me having twins, didn't she? I can't see why she wouldn't believe one of them developed a contagious disease."

Bob was quiet for a minute. "I wish you hadn't claimed the kid had chickenpox. That will keep you home for a week or more. You could have accomplished just as much by claiming he had an upset stomach."

"I was lucky to come up with anything rational, I was so startled by her return."

"Will she want you back?"

"I don't know. I couldn't tell. If that boyfriend of hers hadn't shown up I might have silenced her permanently."

Bob gave her a sharp look. "Isaac wouldn't like that, Thelma. His agents have the right to make that decision, but we don't." Raz stopped for a moment. "I think you should give Ms. Sanderson a call in a couple of days."

"About what?"

"I think," he paused, "you should tell her that you misdiagnosed the red spots your kid had and since they're all gone and he's cleared to go back to school, you can return to work. That way you won't have to miss an entire week. We want you in that office as soon as possible." He looked at her suspiciously. "Lolling around at home due to a fake disease on a kid you don't really have is not helping the cause."

"What exactly am I doing in that office anyway?" She stared at her husband.

"Isaac, or one of his buddies, has the ears I installed." Raz's patience was wearing thin. "But in the event Sanderson is privileged to FBI information, you being in her office might let us know what the FBI suspects. The ears wouldn't necessarily pick up on that."

Tom pulled up at Teddy's house, glad for the chance to take her home. She was still shaking from her encounter with Thelma Rasmussen, but she'd felt like she belonged in his arms. He was looking forward to testing his theory once they were inside. He stopped the car, dashed around to open her door, and together they headed toward her front porch.

Suddenly they stopped.

"My God. What happened?" Tom covered his nose. "Do you have kids in the area?" He was looking at piles of garbage strewn across Teddy's porch.

She shook her head and sighed. "Young kids toss toilet paper in trees. This isn't kids. This is Myron reminding me that he's not far away."

"Myron? How can you be sure?"

"Experience, Tom. I learned through experience."

CHAPTER
19

"Thanks for pulling the Rasmussen files," Tom said to Dillard early the next morning after dropping Teddy off at her office. "Did you look at them?"

"Enough to know both Rasmussens are Alliance members."

Tom scooted forward in his chair. "We've put Teddy in a dangerous spot. We need to get Thelma out of her office."

"No way," Dillard said. "That woman is a good connection to the Alliance. We need her in Teddy's office. One of these days, when she thinks she's alone, she'll phone other Alliance members."

"Do you really think she's dumb enough to do that? From Teddy's phone?"

"You said the look on her face was murderous. If she was stupid enough to consider harming Sanderson, then she might be dumb enough to make personal calls."

"This picture of her husband is interesting," Tom said, studying the photo of Bob Rasmussen. "I'll bet once Teddy sees it she'll recognize him as the man who installed listening devices in her office."

"I don't think you should show it to her just yet. It might make her nervous as hell. You already said she doesn't want his wife anywhere near her, and we're going to ask her to welcome the spy back. That's a lot of stress for someone not in the business." He pulled papers from his filing cabinet.

"We need to get these guys identified and behind bars."

Dillard sat down. "We're making progress. We've installed a honey-pot. That should tempt someone to make unwise choices."

Teddy reluctantly returned to her office Tuesday morning. Tom had picked her up, treated her to a cup of coffee and then dropped his bombshell. Thelma needed to continue as Teddy's secretary.

"She's too valuable for us to let her go," he explained.

"Valuable? Are you saying she's one of the radicals in the Alliance?" When Tom wouldn't say more, Teddy finally resigned herself to the inevitable. It apparently didn't matter how much she mistrusted Thelma or how uneasy she'd feel being alone with her. Thelma was going to be spending hours of each day at her side.

As Teddy dug out her keys to unlock her office, she remembered how she'd felt when she discovered Thelma going through her desk the night before. She shuddered. What surprise awaited her today? She inserted her key and when the deadbolt snapped, she pushed on the door.

It didn't move.

She pushed again, and again the door resisted. For a fleeting moment she was tempted to turn and run. She glanced down the hall in time to see Jed Baxter leaving the elevator.

"Hi Teddy," he called, hurrying toward her. "Is something the matter with your door?"

"If my door won't open, I don't have to go to work. Isn't that right?" Teddy's laugh sounded strained.

"We can't have you goofing off. Let me try."

Jed pushed against the door and slowly it inched open so that Teddy could see the obstruction was due to a newspaper that had been pushed through the mail slot and was wedged under the door.

"Wrestle the door back and forth," Jed suggested.

In a moment she was able to slip through the opening and ease the paper out of the way. "Thanks, Jed," she said.

"Let me know if you need more help," he replied, unlocking the attorney's offices across the hall.

The newspaper, Teddy discovered, had been folded open to page five where a red marking pen had been used to highlight words and underlined phrases. Teddy pulled her gloves from her tote and put them on. If there were any fingerprints, she'd preserved them. She sat down to study the page normally devoted to national news.

Across town Raz and Adam were also studying papers. Theirs were spread across a well-worn table in a modest house owned by Alliance member Lyle Bascom, manager of a magnetic sign shop.

Isaac had suggested Bob and Adam meet because Alliance members were restless. Those financing the group's activities suggested targets, but it was important to have Alliance members think the sites being targeted were selected by their members.

Raz had misgivings about his young colleague's skill. At times Adam seemed reckless. Now, with plans ready to be implemented, it was imperative they agree on an acceptable target.

"I tell you, Raz, no one suspects my skills. They don't know that I provide money, explosives and technical help with hacking."

"That is well and good," Raz responded. "But we still don't have the plans sent to us by Isaac. You must find them."

The words stung Adam. Everyone still blamed him for the lost information. He bent over the diagram they'd been studying. It was of an electrical plant, detailing the facility's complex structure, along with notes that included directions and measurements. It had been supplied by Wendell Green.

"Your group must be sure the detonator gives them time to escape." Adam pointed to a section of the drawing. "But, all this," his finger drew circles over a section of the map, "must be destroyed." Adam looked at Raz to see if he understood.

Bob Rasmussen listened intently to the young man's directions, nodding that he understood the warnings. He liked installing explosives and measuring their destructive power.

The two men continued talking in low voices. It was important to Adam that others in the Alliance believed they were behind the activities planned for the West Coast. It was this group of people, determined to destroy their own country, who needed to be thought of as the originators of the criminal acts. That was essential to the plans of those financing the destruction.

Adam continued, "Have you memorized exactly how you must do this?"

"Of course," Raz assured him impatiently.

"And you will give me the paint to mark the name of your organization?"

"Of course. Everything has been taken care of."

With the morning's crumpled newspaper at her side, Teddy waited for Tom to answer his phone. She felt she understood the message conveyed by the marked up paper: '*I'm watching you. Trouble is on the way.*' That sounded personal enough, but it was the tirade that followed that sounded like the real threat. Something was to be *ignited* in the near future. Did that mean it would be blown up?

Whether the danger was directed at her or at others was a puzzle. The underlined words and phrases didn't give her a clue who might have left the message. Could it have been Thelma Rasmussen, busy with a red pen now that she was no longer searching Teddy's office for who knows what? Teddy realized that at the time she confronted Thelma, she'd been too frightened to wonder what Thelma was really looking for. It couldn't possibly have been a phone number. After all, she'd called Teddy to set up the job interview. She certainly had been able to reach Teddy when she made *that* call. Teddy leaned forward and entered Tom's phone number again.

Could the marked newspaper be the work of Connor Douglas, hoping Teddy would blow it out of proportion so he could get his byline back on page one?

Teddy eased back in her chair to consider the possibilities: Connor Douglas? Thelma Rasmussen? An unidentified burglar? Teddy gave up waiting for Tom to answer his cell phone and called his unlisted number. He picked up promptly.

"What's up?" he asked.

"You're in luck. My schedule has changed and I can have coffee with you now instead of later, if you're still available?" There was anxiety in her voice and she hoped he would hear it. He'd know they hadn't made plans to meet.

"I'm always eager to be with you," Tom responded calmly. "It's a good thing I'm looking for work in your neighborhood. I'll be in your lobby in five minutes."

"Perfect," Teddy said, looking up at the thermostat where a listening device conveyed her every word to unknown listeners. "The lobby it is."

"Perhaps we'll treat ourselves to a short walk and enjoy the gorgeous day," Tom added.

Teddy didn't wait five minutes. She slipped the folded newspaper carefully into her tote, locked her office, and walked quickly to the elevator. In the lobby she paused, pleased when Tom arrived only a few minutes later. He took her arm and briskly walked her out of the building and into the city park across the street.

"What's got you spooked?" he asked, pointing in the direction of a lovely tree with leaves already turning red in the chill October weather. Let anyone watching them assume they were enjoying the day.

"When I walked into my office this morning, I found a copy of today's newspaper pushed through the mail slot." Anxiety was creeping into her voice again. "It was open to page five. Words and phrases are highlighted in red. It's quite a tirade really, but the reason I called you is that it sounds like a threat."

"Stay calm. You're handling it just fine." Tom took her arm and guided her to a bench facing a flower border where colorful fall asters were grouped behind late-blooming marigolds. "Is the message clearly threatening or is it one you've read too much into?"

"It rambles," Teddy agreed and added, "It begins, '*I'm watching you. Trouble is on its way.*' Or something like that." Teddy scuffed her toe against the paving. "It goes on about the revolution about to take place and threatens to ignite something to show that I can't stop them. Who would send such a message?" She faced Tom. "Who or what is it that I can't stop?" Her voice was tight.

"We can analyze that later. Do you have the newspaper with you?"

Teddy nodded.

"Don't hand it to me. Let's take a turn around the park and when we're near that group of trees…," Tom nodded in the direction of a small grove of alders, "you can plant a little lipstick on my face as you slip me the newspaper. I'll take it upstairs and have it analyzed and fingerprinted. We'll see what the experts can tell us about whether there's a real threat." When Teddy nodded, he took her arm and helped her up. They walked into the small grove of alders. "Now for the lipstick part of this meeting, in the name of justice, of course."

"At least a smudge," she said.

"Why else would we walk into a stand of alders if it wasn't to share a kiss? I'll be wiping lipstick from my face when we emerge. Anyone watching will assume that's why we ducked into the trees." Tom looked at his serious companion and laughed. "You might try smiling a little so anyone watching will think you are enjoying this little rendezvous."

With a smile, Teddy took Tom's arm and playfully pulled him more deeply into the small grove. The newspaper was safely transferred from her tote to his inside coat pocket as she leaned against him and left a blurry bit of lipstick on his cheek. He was scrubbing at it when they emerged from the trees. Teddy was flushed, but smiling.

He caught her look and said, "Not to worry. Your big brother is on the case." He pulled his horn-rimmed glasses from a pocket and put them on, trying to look business-like.

Teddy studied his face, knowing that a little knot of fear had settled in her heart. Despite what he said, she couldn't make it go away.

CHAPTER
20

The weekend Connor Douglas spent with his out-of-town friend had been unexpectedly boring. It had taken him a while to get over his jitters about someone searching his apartment, but now, back in the city, he had plans he wanted to put in motion. To start with, he called Detection Systems and asked them to install new locking devices on his apartment door. Having done that, he hurried from his apartment to talk with the building manager.

Greg was surprised when Connor informed him of his plan to change the locks on his door. "None of the other tenants feel the need for added security," Greg said. But after a long conversation, he reluctantly gave Connor permission, as long as keys for his new locks were left at the office.

An hour after Connor left for work, a white truck with a sign that said *Thompson Security Systems* pulled into the lot. The curly-haired man wearing a uniform that said *Thompson's* on the pocket stopped at the manager's office, and asked for the key to Connor's apartment. After repeating Connor's instructions for new locks almost word for word, he was allowed into the apartment. The door closed quietly behind the busy apartment manager, and when it did, Adam opened his tool box and immediately got to work.

###

Back at the newspaper office Connor was berating himself for being forgetful. He'd installed his own surveillance in the apartment before he'd left for the boring weekend with friends. The system was relatively invisible next to his smoke detector. This morning he'd been so excited about getting new locks, he forgot to check the memory card in the surveillance camera.

Back in his car, he headed home. As he drove into the complex, he noticed the Thompson Security Systems truck, and laughed. The apartment manager had said no one else felt the need to increase their security, but apparently that wasn't the case. He'd hired Detection Systems, but someone else had obviously called Thompson. Eager to watch his cantankerous friend eat his words, Connor detoured to the manager's office.

"Hi Greg," Connor said, stepping into the office.

"Hi yourself, Connor," Greg responded. "That fly-by-night security company you hired showed up quick enough, but I'm surprised you didn't hire Detection Systems. They've got the best reputation in town."

Connor studied Greg's face to see if he was kidding. "You let the Thompson people into my apartment?" He took a deep breath.

"Of course. You told me to."

"And they're installing the new locks now?"

Greg nodded. "They should be nearly finished and bringing me your new keys. Why don't you go on up and get them yourself?"

"Can't," Connor said, turning back to the door. He rushed to his car, grabbed his cell phone and called the company with whom he'd placed his order.

"Detection Systems," answered the company's receptionist.

"This is Connor Douglas. About an hour ago I placed an order for new locks on my apartment door. I should have asked when you expected to do the job."

"We can't get there before the day after tomorrow," the receptionist replied. "Will that be soon enough?"

"Do you ever hand off jobs to other companies?" He took out a handkerchief and mopped his sweating face.

"Never."

"Not even Thompson Security Systems?"

"Hold on a minute, Mr. Douglas."

Connor could hear the receptionist consulting with someone in the office. Finally she came back to the phone. "We've never even heard of the company you mentioned. Is there anything else we can do for you?"

"No. I'll see you in a couple of days." Connor hung up and grabbed his camera. He photographed the white van from all angles, then went to the front windshield and checked the vehicle identification number. It had been covered up. Running back to his car, he got in, drove out of the lot, and parked down the street. He was breathing hard.

If someone was in his apartment installing new locks, or more likely searching it, then two things seemed probable. There must be a microphone of some kind already hidden in his apartment, and as soon as he could get to his spy camera, he should be able to see exactly what the intruder had been doing. Once the bogus locksmith left, Connor intended to follow him.

When Teddy returned to her office after meeting Tom in the park, she found Jed Baxter waiting at her door.

He greeted her enthusiastically. "Am I ever glad to see you."

Teddy laughed. "I suppose you want to borrow a cup of sugar?"

"What?" Surprise wrinkled Jed's forehead.

"Come in and have a seat, Jed," Teddy invited. "I was trying to make a joke."

"Oh, I see." Frowning again, the young attorney followed Teddy into her office and promptly sat in her client chair.

"What can I do for you?" She lowered herself into the chair behind her desk.

"My boss, Ed Booker, has several cases he needs help with. Since you're a paralegal, we're turning some of the work over to you." He lowered his voice. "I've got to be honest with you though." Jed pulled folders from his briefcase and handed them to her. "Ed likes lots of detail and lots of follow up. He's like the Internal Revenue Service when it does an audit—the more paperwork you supply, the happier he is."

"Thanks for the tip, Jed. I'll give his work my best shot. Do you want to leave the records with me, or should I make copies and give them back to you?"

"Those are copies I made for you."

"That was very thoughtful." She glanced through the folders. "If you can wait a minute I'd like to scan the material to see if I have questions."

Jed nodded and sat quietly, watching Teddy carefully examine the first folder. It was obvious she had an eye for meticulous detail.

"The Torgeson matter looks like all it needs is a land surveyor to establish the property boundaries, and then a timber cruiser to establish value." She looked up. "Is that what Mr. Booker has in mind?"

"Perfect," Jed said approvingly. "You'll want to walk the property yourself, of course. Do some personal follow up just to make sure the litigants haven't already approached the surveyors with a bribe."

"Of course," she replied, opening the next folder. "I see in the Dixon matter you're looking for witnesses to a traffic accident that put your client in the hospital."

Jed stood up and stretched. "I think you'll do a fine job," he said, smiling broadly. "Stay in touch and keep records of your time and expenses." He handed Teddy a business card on which he'd written a number. "I'll be your contact for these cases, so if you have any questions call me at any time. I'm seldom in court. Oh," he reached into his breast pocket. "I'm also authorized to give you an advance." He handed a check to Teddy just as her phone rang.

"Thanks, Jed. I'll get right on these." She patted the stack of files and reached for the phone.

He waved as he left. "Call me tonight," he said, pausing at the door.

Teddy nodded. "If I have questions," she said, picking up her phone. "Girl Friday, Sanderson speaking."

"Hi, Teddy!" Tom said. "Are you hungry? Ready for lunch?"

"I'm not sure I have the time," she said. "I have some new work so I'll be busy for a while."

"We can make it a quick lunch. How about I pick you up in a few minutes? In the lobby."

Teddy laughed. "How quick will lunch be?"

"Perfect response," Tom replied. "See you in the lobby in five minutes."

CHAPTER
21

Tom left the Stettler Building with Teddy running beside him. "This won't take long," he promised. "How big was the advance Baxter gave you?"

"How did you know?" She looked at him, suddenly understanding. "I see. It isn't just the bad guys bugging my office, is it? Your team installed hardware, too." Tom's raised eyebrow was all the confirmation she needed. "Five hundred dollars."

Tom took her arm and walked her across the street, and into the park. They sat on the first bench they found. He opened the sack he'd been carrying. "Tuna salad or bologna?"

"Where did these sandwiches come from?" Teddy reached for the tuna and took a bite.

"The bologna is mine. Dilly contributed the tuna."

"Dilly?"

"Dillard. My boss."

"Thank him for me. This is good." She smiled, smacked her lips, and took another bite. "Why are we sharing borrowed sandwiches?" She reached for the other half of her tuna sandwich.

"It's because of your newspaper. We think we know what it means."

"Go ahead."

"We don't think it's directed at you, other than as a person who was present when an FBI agent died. We're leaning toward it being a warning that the Alliance is about to become active again."

"I'm glad to know I'm not in any personal danger." She took the last bite of her sandwich and folded the wax paper that had been wrapped around it.

"There's more."

"I might have known." She stared at him as she continued chewing.

"As I told you the other day, we have the recording Sam intercepted. We're putting together one of our own to take its place." Tom looked at Teddy, scanning her face for signs of anxiety. "We're assuming the Alliance has enough layers to their organization that they aren't able to recognize every voice."

"Do you know where Sam picked up their communication?"

"Not yet."

Teddy said, "I came back here after his death, trying to recall things going on around me that day as I walked through the park."

"And?"

"And I realized I'd seen the man who later said he was a secret agent. He was sitting on this bench. I remembered thinking how lucky he was to be relaxing in the park. He wore sunglasses."

"I wish we could find him." Tom stood, ready to return to work.

Teddy got to her feet. "I realized I'd seen Sam jaywalking from the Stettler toward the park. What puzzles me is the timing. There was only a minute, maybe two, between Sam running toward this park, and him dying on the other side of the street."

"Until you reported to Dillard, we weren't sure how long Sam was out of his office. For all we knew he was attacked as he exited the building that morning."

"I don't think that's what happened. I think he left the building and jaywalked across the street to this park because he was in a hurry. What I don't understand is where he found the CD or who delivered the fatal wound." They fell silent. "I think the so-called *special agent* searched Sam's pockets because he was hunting for whatever it was Sam intercepted." Teddy wadded the neatly folded sandwich papers and twisted them together with the crumpled lunch sack. "Did Connor tell you about the other man that day? The one he thought was communicating with the so-called *special agent*?"

"He did. We don't have any leads on that guy either." Tom balled up the papers that had held his bologna sandwich, and pitched them into the garbage can. "Two points," he declared.

"From Connor's description and that of my neighbor, I think the pizza deliveryman could be the person Connor saw that day." Teddy turned toward the garbage can and pitched her sandwich bag. She missed and the bag landed on the sidewalk beside the empty can.

"I'm not picking you for *my* basketball team," Tom laughed. He walked to the can and bent to retrieve the paper from the graffiti-marked paving, then froze.

"Are you all right?" Teddy asked, taking a step toward him.

He put his hand on the small of his back, then grasped Teddy's arm. "Do me a favor."

"Of course."

"Stand right where you are for five full minutes. Don't move. After five minutes you can return to your office."

"What's going on?"

"I'll explain later. Five full minutes." With that, Tom rushed across the street amid honking horns and motorists swerving to avoid him.

Bursting into the FBI reception area, Tom dashed through the doorway and headed for his boss's office. He grabbed Dillard's arm. "Come," he gasped, short of breath. "Hurry!"

Dillard followed Tom into Sam's office. They stood beside the windows. "What are we looking at?" Dillard asked.

"Teddy. In the park. See? Beside the can."

"Catch your breath and then make sense." Dillard started to move from the windows, but Tom grabbed his arm and pinned him next to the glass.

"No, look! See Teddy?"

"I see her. She just looked at her watch. Now she's at the corner, waiting for the light to change."

"Take Sam's binoculars," Tom blurted, pointing to binoculars on the windowsill. "Look where she was standing. Tell me what you see."

Dillard adjusted the binoculars. "There's a bench with one of those chained garbage cans beside it. The can looks fairly empty."

"Lower," Tom demanded. "Look at the paving in front of the can."

Obediently Dillard adjusted the magnification. "My God!" he gasped, swallowing a deep breath. "That's how Sam knew."

Teddy gave up wondering about Tom and his five minute instructions as she made another entry in the Smith file and prepared the accompanying report. With Sally Anne the only beneficiary on life insurance policies her husband hadn't purchased, it seemed clear she was planning his demise. Unfortunately, William's present condition made him vulnerable, even with a nurse and a bodyguard around him. The driver suspected of trying to kill William, Wendell Green, was being questioned by police. Teddy leaned back in her chair. She had six cases to work on for Attorney Booker, and so far today she hadn't heard from Connor or Thelma. Life was really very good.

As she prepared to leave the office, her phone rang. "Girl Friday, Sanderson speaking."

"Miss Sanderson, this is Thelma Rasmussen."

Teddy considered hanging up.

"You said I could be in touch once Cole was better. We've just returned from the doctor's office." Thelma paused. "He has hives, not chickenpox. It's only an allergy."

"Well, that's good news, isn't it?" Teddy wished she could tell this woman to jump in the lake.

"It's wonderful. It means he can return to school tomorrow and Cameron won't catch anything. I thought," she paused, her voice tentative, "if you still want me, I can return to work tomorrow."

"Perfect," Teddy lied, wishing the FBI hadn't asked her to let Thelma back into her office. "I have new assignments so there's typing and other things you can do. That will help me a lot."

"You won't be sorry you hired me," Thelma responded.

###

Connor Douglas stood beside the telephone in the Stettler lobby. He'd just placed a call to the fifth floor. It was time he met with the FBI's top hotshot. If he told all he knew or suspected, the FBI would take over and things would be out of his control. But with the leverage he had now, if he bargained with the top guy, they'd have to see they had no choice but to include him in whatever was going on. They'd at least have to promise him an exclusive on the story.

"Mr. Douglas?" The woman stopping beside him had plain features and glasses pushed to the top of her head. "Agent Brighton is waiting for you."

Connor followed her into the elevator and watched her insert her key card. Once on the fifth floor, she ushered him to Brighton's office.

Dillard gestured Connor to a chair and asked, "What can I do for you?"

The next morning Teddy wound her way through traffic. The uneasy feeling in the pit of her stomach was becoming familiar. Somewhere close, Myron was setting up who knew what. She didn't doubt for one minute he was plotting to kill her.

And then there was Thelma. Teddy's stomach gave another lurch. If Tom hadn't insisted, she'd have fired Thelma on the spot. She would probably never know what the woman had been looking for the night Teddy discovered her going through things.

Teddy pulled into the underground parking garage, and a moment later headed for her office, still puzzling over Connor's story in the morning paper. It mentioned the marked newspaper threat Teddy received and made reference to a *recently released video* which was sure to interfere with terrorist plans.

Teddy hadn't heard of any recently released video. What was he talking about? Was this more of the FBI's misinformation? She sighed, and unlocked her office door.

###

Adam had been brooding all morning over Isaac's lack of trust. The lost information had to be found. He knew that. He knew, too, that he needed to find it to prove he was able to participate at higher levels of the Alliance's plans.

As he raced from his apartment in his running suit, he didn't notice the car containing Myron Ratini heading in the opposite direction. Nor did he notice it waiting near the magnetic sign lot when he reached his van. Adam entered the van, then emerged wearing his white technician's uniform. He pulled out the business card he'd stolen, and called the number.

"Girl Friday, Sanderson speaking," said the voice in his ear.

Adam smiled and hung up. If she was at work then he could search her empty house.

Much to Teddy's surprise and relief, the morning went quite well. Thelma arrived on time and the new cases provided more than enough work to keep both women busy. Teddy looked at her watch. It was almost lunch time. She needed to head to the library for information on Attorney Ed Booker's cases. She glanced at Thelma, bent over her desk.

"Thelma, I need to go to the library to do some research. It's nearly lunch time. Why don't you go to lunch and meet me back here at one?"

Thelma nodded. "It'll only take me a minute to finish this letter. Then I'll follow you out."

Teddy gave her an inquiring look. She still didn't trust this woman. The phone rang. "Girl Friday, Sanderson speaking."

"It's Tom. Meet me at the library as soon as possible. Okay?"

"Okay." She looked back at Thelma, still finishing a letter. "I'm on my way to the library. Lock up when you finish that letter. I'll see you back here at one."

Thelma waited at the window behind her desk, watching for Teddy's car to leave the basement parking. When it reached the street and turned toward the city library, Thelma locked the office door.

It was exactly the opportunity she'd been hoping for. Hurrying to Teddy's file cabinet, she thumbed through it, scanning for names she recognized. The sound of someone at the locked door jiggling the doorknob interrupted her. The jiggling was followed by a knock. Thelma quickly shut the file drawer, grabbed her purse and moved across the room to open the door.

"Mr. Heeter," she greeted the man standing in the doorway. "I was just leaving for lunch." She turned to get her coat. "Ms. Sanderson is at the library, but if there's something I can help you with…."

Tom walked past Thelma as she struggled into her coat. "I'm returning this." He put a CD on Teddy's desk. "I already have one like this." He smiled. "Make sure Teddy sees it when she returns. Tell her I said thanks, but she's free to pass this on to someone else."

"I'll give her your message." Thelma glanced at the CD. It read, *The Sound of Music* and had a small mark on the label near the word *music*. She inhaled a sharp breath. What luck! Could this be what everyone was searching for?

"Well, I'm off," Tom said, heading for the door. "Don't let Teddy make you work too long. Take time for lunch!"

Thelma nodded. Sixty seconds after the door shut behind Tom, Thelma locked it and was on the phone. "I've got it, Bob. I've got the CD!"

"What're you talking about?" Raz responded in irritation.

She whispered, "The recording everybody's been looking for; the one the FBI agent stole!"

"Describe it," Raz said, then a moment later added, "That's it. Put it in your purse and get out of there. I'll be outside the building in fifteen minutes."

Thelma looked at the clock. Teddy was due back at one and would be expecting to find her waiting outside the locked door. "All right, but get here right away. I'm to meet Sanderson at one. If I'm late, she'll be upset."

"I'm on my way."

Thelma expected to meet Bob in fifteen minutes. That gave her time to make a few calls. Grabbing her purse, she pulled out a small purple address book. The names in it were disguises for Alliance members and the numbers themselves were coded. She picked up the receiver and with corrections, dialed the number beside Nancy's name. The ringing phone didn't reach anyone named Nancy. On the second ring a man answered. Thelma smiled and began sharing her good news.

CHAPTER
22

Bob Rasmussen slammed the car door as he got out. He didn't like hurrying and he'd just realized his wife would need a replacement for the CD she planned to give him. He had barely enough time to purchase one and still meet her before the one o'clock deadline.

After the exchange he headed home, eager to listen to the document that had been stolen by the FBI agent. As he entered the house, he heard his phone and grabbed it. "Hello," he shouted into the receiver.

"It's Lyle. I can't join you tomorrow."

"I don't understand," Bob said. "What's going on?"

"My wife had a baby three days ago, and she's having difficulty— the baby, not my wife. We've already made one rush trip to the hospital. Susan's very upset and I can't leave her. You'll have to get someone to fill in for me."

"You're the only one with explosives experience. We need you." Bob's voice was hoarse.

"I'm not leaving Susan's side." Silence hung heavy in the air. Finally Lyle said, "How about the fellow who sets up our projects? The one who leaves his truck in my sign yard? He must know something about how things need to be finalized."

"Adam doesn't want to be involved beyond the communication phase. His part is to identify a project and get the information and supplies to us. He never participates in the hands-on part of an operation."

"Explain the situation to him. See if he can't assist this once. We all need to get our hands dirty now and then." Lyle sounded tired but unyielding.

Bob ran nervous fingers through his thinning hair. He could tell there was no use arguing. "I'll talk to him," he said, and slammed the receiver in its cradle. He lit a cigarette and considered the skills of those in the Alliance group. Tomorrow's mission couldn't wait. Timing was everything. The power plant's computer system had been hacked, and night security should be at a minimum due to a flu outbreak. It was the perfect time for the Alliance to strike.

Bob ground his cigarette stub in the ashtray and considered Adam. He was in this country with fake ID, so having him take part in an operation that might bring him to the attention of law enforcement was risky. If he was deported, it would be disastrous for the Alliance. He'd been an electrical engineer in his own country, so he had the training. The question was *did he have the courage to take part?*

Bob picked up the phone and punched in numbers.

Adam's line was busy. He was on the phone, talking with Mario. "What do you mean?" he yelled in panic, navigating his truck down a busy side street.

"I said I'm leaving. I'm headed home to train others."

"But Mario, we're a team! You are still training me!"

"Isaac thinks you can handle things alone. It's a vote of confidence." Mario sounded tired. "He trusts you to continue our work."

"I cannot do it. I failed to recover our plans. The red-haired one doesn't have them. I am on my way to the woman's house to search it again."

"The information that was stolen has been recovered. Bob Rasmussen has it and that's where we wanted it to end up. The Alliance can move forward now, with you leading them."

Adam tried to control his growing panic. "I do not think you taught me the skills needed to lead."

"Oh, come on, Adam. You'll do just fine." A background noise interrupted Mario. "They're calling my flight. I have to go." The line went dead.

Adam listened to the dial tone. What would he do without Mario? He slipped his cell phone into a shirt pocket and it immediately began ringing. He pulled it out and punched the receive mode. A wave of relief swept over him. "Mario?"

"No. It's Raz."

Adam's heart sank and his feelings of panic returned. It was true then. Mario had gone home.

Adam swerved to avoid a driver's car door opening into his lane of traffic.

He said, "I am told you have the lost information."

"I just got it! We can go forward with our plans now, so get over here."

"I'm on my way," Adam replied, quickly negotiating a U-turn.

"We have one important change," Raz continued. "Our engineer has dropped out. You will be taking his place."

"No! I cannot be your engineer."

"We'll discuss that when you get here."

Adam sat in stunned silence, listening to another dial tone, his foot resting heavily on the gas pedal. His hands shook and he was unaware of flashing lights and a siren drawing closer.

Because Thelma didn't have a key to Teddy's office, she left the door unlocked when she raced down the stairs to switch CDs with Bob. She barely had time to return to the office, leave the replacement CD on Teddy's desk, and pull the door shut before Teddy showed up to unlock it.

"Did you have a good lunch?" Teddy inquired, unlocking the recently locked door.

"I had to hurry," Thelma said, breathing hard as they entered the office. "But I'm ready to get back to work."

"Perfect," Teddy said. She pulled a rotary card file from the bag she was carrying. "I need names and addresses from the six new cases on this card file. I'd also like a listing of them in my computer." She took a deep breath. "Any questions about how to set it up?"

Thelma shook her head. "Your friend Tom came by with a CD that he put on your desk." Thelma motioned to the recording. "He said you'd given it to him, and he was returning it because he has one exactly like it. He said you could pass it on to someone else."

"It's yours if you want it," Teddy replied, gathering a few items from her desk and heading back to the door. "I have an arrangement just like that one. Now then, I have an appointment, so I'll see you later." With a wave she headed down the hall to the elevator. When it stopped its only occupant was Agent Brighton's secretary. She smiled a greeting at Teddy and with her pass card, delivered Teddy to the fifth floor.

"Now that we're all here," Dillard said as Teddy took a seat, "let's go over recent findings." Tom Heeter and a smug-looking Connor Douglas were already seated.

Teddy frowned. "What's he doing here?" she asked nodding at Connor. "Why do we need a reporter?"

The smile left Connor's face. He looked embarrassed.

Dillard nodded at Tom. "Bring Sanderson up-to-date, Agent Heeter."

"It's this way, Teddy," Tom began. "Connor recently supplied us with some terrific information, so he's been added to the team. In addition, while you were at the library this noon, I gave the CD our experts prepared to your secretary."

"She offered it to me," Teddy said. "I told her it was hers if she wanted it."

"Actually she was very busy while you were gone. The disk she offered you isn't the one I gave her. She handed that one off to her husband, and he gave her a replacement. Dilly, show Rasmussen's picture to Teddy."

Dillard sorted papers on his desk, and then handed a picture to Teddy.

"That's him," she exclaimed, nearly jumping from her chair. "That's the man who put listening devices in my office, claiming to be Donald Kennedy."

"We figured as much," Dillard said, reclaiming the photo. "He's married to your secretary."

Tom continued, "Before the recording changed hands today, Thelma made phone calls to Alliance members, bragging about how *she's* the one who recovered the CD Isaac sent."

"Miss Sanderson," Dillard broke in. "We'd like you to give Thelma a key to your office. If she can't be alone in it once in a while, she won't call other Alliance members. Thanks to her we're getting a very nice index of those in the organization. As soon as we can nail down the group's top contacts, we'll arrest the whole bunch."

Teddy started to voice her objection, but Tom cut her off. "We know your work is often sensitive. We'll provide you with a special cabinet for your use until this investigation is over. Okay?"

She frowned, but nodded. "I'll give Thelma a key as soon as this meeting's over. Okay?"

Dillard said, "We expect to close down the group fairly soon if the Alliance falls for our sweet honeypot."

Teddy looked puzzled.

"It's a fake control computer we set up to lure criminals into cyber traps. As for Connor's part in all of this," he nodded at the young man, "he supplied us with pictures." Dillard clicked buttons on his desk and a screen came down from the ceiling. "Will you catch the lights, Tom?"

When the room darkened, Dillard said, "Connor, for Sanderson's benefit, explain what we're seeing."

A white van advertising *Thompson Security Systems* showed up on the screen, and Connor said, "Yesterday I called Detection Systems and asked them to change my apartment locks. I headed to work, and then remembered I'd forgotten to unload my hidden camera. When I got back to the apartment I discovered this truck in the parking lot and asked my apartment manager about it. He said he thought that was the company I'd hired, so he gave them the keys to my apartment.

"I photographed the truck, then parked down the street and waited for its driver to show up. When he did, I followed him." A magnetic sign yard showed up next. "The man I followed parked his van here. The owner of the sign company has to be another Alliance member. The guy I was following changed into running clothes and headed to his apartment." The picture of an apartment complex came next. "This place is on Kentucky Avenue and the van driver lives in number 312. He's registered as Adam Baily.

"I brought this film to Agent Brighton yesterday, and he sent Agent Heeter with me to sweep my apartment. As I suspected, a listening device had been installed. That's how the Thompson people knew I'd hired someone to change my locks.

"Tom and I recovered the memory card from the camera I'd installed and it showed this guy searching my apartment." The film they watched showed a dark, curly-haired man searching Connor's apartment. "He drives the Thompson's truck, and he's the man who was standing behind you," he nodded at Teddy, "when Sam Morgan died."

Teddy said, "Look at his hair and his face. I bet he's the man my neighbor has seen breaking into my house."

Tom said, "He is. We already checked with Mrs. Plummer."

Teddy responded, "And C. Bradford, the crime reporter Connor can't seem to locate, is he putting all of this in his column tomorrow?"

Connor ducked his head and wouldn't meet Teddy's gaze.

Dillard shook his head. "Connor is our media contact. He'll release only information we approve, and not one thing more." Dillard frowned at Connor. "Understood? No hints of any kind unless we approve them. And definitely nothing more about Sanderson."

Connor squirmed in his chair. "I've already promised to run everything past you before I give it to the copy editors."

"See that you do."

Tom added, "We think it was Adam who murdered Sam Morgan."

"If Adam is the killer and you arrest him, will I be able to spend weekends alone?" Teddy asked.

Dillard looked first at Tom and then at Teddy. He laughed. "I'm sorry to say that isn't possible. If we've done a good job creating a fake recording, the Alliance will think they have theirs back. But if they discover what they have is a fake, they may come after you or Connor. We can't protect you unless your environment is controlled."

Tom added, "You are most vulnerable at home. Since we're monitoring activities in your office, probably no one will try anything there. It's your time at home we're concerned with."

The phone on Dillard's desk rang three times before Dillard picked it up. "Helen, I asked you not to interrupt," he said, but as he listened, a smile crossed his face. "Tell them to follow, but keep in the background."

The group looked expectantly at Dillard.

"And Helen, thanks for interrupting." Dillard turned, smiling at the group. "City cops just ticketed Adam Bailey for speeding and making an illegal U-turn. They're tracking him for us. They got curious about him when they discovered someone else is following him."

CHAPTER
23

Adam parked his truck in front of a narrow, two-story tan house set back from the street. The house was in a quiet neighborhood of small, well-kept homes, each with tall trees shading their yards. This residence had a blue camper with a bull bar parked in the driveway. Adam climbed the steps to the building's green door, and paused.

It was the first quiet moment he'd had since the traffic stop by city police. He was worried about the ticket's consequences, and he needed time to think about his conversations with Bob Rasmussen and Mario. He stared at the green door, finally giving it three firm raps followed by a pause and then one last rap.

The door swung open. "Come in, come in," Bob Rasmussen greeted. "We've been waiting for you."

Adam hesitated, wiping sweat from his forehead. Bob opened the door wider. "You're the last to arrive. Let's get started."

When Adam stepped into the house, the green door slammed shut behind him.

###

"Now what?" said the man who'd been following Adam. Myron Ratini peeked out from behind trees near the tan house, and then ducked into shrubs lining one side of it. He moved slowly, hoping to overhear whatever was going on inside. He found a window partly opened, and paused. The voices were low, but distinct. He hunched down to listen, unaware that two Whittington policemen were watching him.

"What do you make of that?" one of the city policemen asked his buddy.

"We're supposed to follow, not interfere," his partner replied. "I'll phone in this address and the Accord's license number. Let's see what happens next."

Adam sat in a straight-backed chair, still upset and uncertain. "Before we start, could I have some coffee?" He needed time to assess the men gathered around him. Other than Raz, there was a beefy man with a dark beard resting on his chest, a young man of college age, and two well-dressed businessmen in their early thirties.

Raz handed Adam a cup of coffee, and said, "Now that everyone's here, we can go over our plans for tomorrow night." He turned to the group, "Since our engineer can't join us, Adam will take over as team leader. He'll identify key places to install explosives and do the final check on timing devices." Raz nodded at Adam.

The nervous young man set his coffee aside and surveyed the group. He swiped once at sweat running down his face. "You have all taken part in other Alliance projects, so tomorrow's visit to a power plant will be different only in the amount of explosive material you'll each carry. The timing devices will be set for the same time so we'll have an enormous release of energy when they explode.

"As for specific details regarding disguises, if you have questions, ask them now." Adam searched the men's faces and when no one spoke, he moved to the power plant map on Bob's wall. He began assigning specific locations.

Myron was amazed by what he heard. Talk about being ripe for blackmail! He would attach himself to Adam like a second skin, and as soon as he could get him alone, he'd tell him what the score really was. Myron eased away from the tan house and returned to the black Accord.

Early the next morning Adam's doorbell woke him. He slipped on a robe and hurried to the door. A stranger stood outside the door, cups of coffee in both hands. "Yes?" Adam said.

Myron pushed his way past Adam and kicked the door shut behind him. "I thought we should get better acquainted, Adam, since we're going to be business partners." He handed two coffees to Adam, noting the man's hands trembling and his eyes shifting nervously from side to side. "Give one of those coffees to your wife, and then get back in here so we can talk."

Adam disappeared into his bedroom, but soon returned. "Are you the police?" He sat down, spilling coffee on the rented sofa.

"I'm not the police. I don't want to see them any more than you do, so hear me out." Myron straddled a chair, wiggling until he got comfortable. Then he began. "I know you've searched the office and home of a woman named Teddy Sanderson, and of a reporter for the *News Telegrapher*. I know that yesterday you met with a group of men at the home of Bob Rasmussen, and that you discussed blowing up a power plant tonight. Any corrections so far?"

Adam sat quietly on the sofa, visibly trembling.

"No corrections?" Myron glanced around, noting scruffy items that looked like they belonged in a yard sale. He continued, "I don't plan to interfere with your sabotage as long as I'm not a victim. But I want something in exchange for my silence. I want my ex-wife to be one of your casualties. Do you understand the word *casualty*? I want Teddy Sanderson eliminated, and I want you to be the one to do her in. Knock her off." He stared at Adam. "You will do this on a day I select. And you'll do it at a time I choose. Do we understand each other?"

"I'd like to know more about your ex-husband," Agent Brighton prompted Teddy. "Agent Heeter reports he's rarely seen, but we've learned he's been following a Delphi Alliance member. I've already talked to Myron's parole officer, but I'd like your feedback."

Teddy said, "If he's following an Alliance member it isn't because of any political aspirations. It would be for some other reason. Only a small percentage of whatever Myron's doing is easy to spot. The fact that we haven't seen much of him doesn't mean he's looking for a job or building a better life for himself. It means that until he's ready to spring a trap, all preparations for it are being done quietly and under wraps. He's been out of prison ten or eleven days now. That's probably long enough for him to figure out what he plans to do and to get his alibi set up."

"Do you think his actions will involve you?"

Teddy nodded. "Of course. I think his phone calls, the garbage he left on my porch, and the times my neighbor has seen him at my home, probably mean I need to keep looking over my shoulder."

"If anything happens to you, he'd better have one damn fine alibi or he'll have the FBI staking him to an ant hill."

Teddy grimaced. "That's a delightful picture—Myron and the ant hill, but you're right about one thing; whatever he has planned for me will only happen when he has an airtight alibi. I think it may be time for me to find out when he's next scheduled to meet with his parole officer. Half a dozen years ago I was lucky to avoid his attempts on my life. This time I can't rely on luck alone."

With the onset of night, Adam began preparations for the destruction of the Peoples Power Plant. Like other team members, he dressed in black, slipped a ski mask over his face, and put black gloves in his pocket. He had reviewed with the group exactly what needed to happen, when it needed to happen, and which of them would be responsible for it happening. The men were experienced and ready but Adam was still nervous. His hands shook—not a good thing for the man carrying explosive devices. The best part of tonight's operation would be the satisfaction of knowing the Alliance was playing into the hands of the organization that had sent him to this country.

"The Americans are naive fools," he whispered as he thought of the Alliance members. "They are pawns."

It was unfortunate that the night's plans had been discovered by the man who brought coffee that morning. That stranger could have stopped the attack, but he wanted the death of a woman as payment for his silence. Adam shrugged his shoulders. He'd be able to take care of her. Probably her death would matter very little to anyone. The bigger picture was the need for tonight's activities to go forward without interference.

As Adam headed toward the rendezvous spot he realized that a dark cloud had covered the moon. It was most certainly a sign that the night's activities were being blessed.

Also getting ready for the Alliance's activities was a beefy man with a dark beard. He was driving a blue rig with a bull bar winch attached to its front bumper. His *old woman* had first asked him to do away with her spouse, but when that attempt failed, she suggested Wendell destroy the company her husband was involved in as Chairman of the Board of Directors. Wendell didn't understand how the destruction of the power plant would benefit her, but if Sally Anne wanted something, he always did his best to see that she got whatever it was.

CHAPTER
24

The Peoples Power Plant was in an isolated section of Whittington's industrial park. The dimly-lit east-west road leading to it didn't stop there, but continued west toward a sparsely occupied countryside where small farms were maintained.

Adam parked his dark sedan a block from the plant and turned off the engine. He flicked a red LED light once. At a distance, similar lights flashed, signaling Alliance members were in place.

Adam left his car carrying a soft dark case of timed incendiary devices. As he approached the target, dark shapes emerged from the shadows and followed him. One, the lookout, stayed behind to sound an alarm if anyone approached or if their police scanner signaled problems. Security guards engaged in a bit of gin rummy were tased, then bound and gagged. They'd be unfortunate casualties.

The men entering the plant had two-way radios hanging from their belts. Each carried full propane canisters. Adam handed each an incendiary device as the men headed for specific areas: the boiler unit, the combustion turbines, the generator, the pump, a condenser. The maps they'd studied the previous night proved accurate, allowing them to quickly set up their canisters and timing devices.

Adam checked the strategic positions, his heart galloping as he did so. When everyone finished and drove away, he walked to a shed at the edge of the property and with a spray can of red paint wrote: *Delphi*

Alliance. He returned to his car and headed east, turning his headlights on when he felt safe. He didn't need another traffic ticket, especially not tonight and not in this location. Checking his speedometer, he drove through the night, back to his apartment and his bed.

When he awoke the next morning, the house was silent and Yolinda was asleep beside him. He raised his head to glance at the bedside clock, but he couldn't read it. He stretched to turn on the reading lamp, and when it didn't work, he smiled. That meant their plan had succeeded.

In the western section of the city where power was provided by Western Power and Light, Teddy Sanderson awoke and reached to shut off her alarm. In the kitchen she started a pot of coffee, and then took a shower, hurrying through her morning routine.

She turned on the television to listen to the morning news and was greeted by a crawler moving across the bottom of the screen. *Breaking News. An explosion at Peoples Power Plant has disrupted power for most of Whittington. Area cell towers were also destroyed. The Delphi Alliance claims responsibility. One death is confirmed.*

Teddy snapped off the television. The Peoples Power Plant? That was William Smith's company. Had Sally Anne gotten her friend Wendell Green to assist the Alliance in destroying the structure? Supplying the extremists with a fake CD hadn't stopped them. What would it take?

While the Stettler Building was without power, a back-up generator kicked in on the FBI's fifth floor.

"Chalk one up for the Alliance," muttered Dillard Brighton to the men assembled in his office. He paced the floor as he spoke. "I thought we were on top of that group's activities, but obviously we weren't."

"Come on, Dilly. We all heard their CD. What if they'd taken out the facilities mentioned there?" Tom Heeter handed his friend a cup of coffee.

"We've got to get that group shut down," Dillard said. "The most promising lead we have is the one supplied by Thelma Rasmussen, but for the time being, that's dried up." He growled, "With cell towers down and no service, she can't contact her buddies."

"We know now that her husband is more than a sympathizer," Tom added. "He has to be one of the local kingpins." Tom looked at Buford Jackson. "What about Isaac and Mario??"

Agent Jackson shifted in his seat. "We have surveillance tapes showing Mario at the airport. He must have known about last night's plans and left this area ahead of time. As for Isaac, we don't think he's ever been in this country. He seems to call the shots from a distance, usually by cell phone."

Dillard smiled for the first time that morning. "Do you mean Adam and his wife are here without supervision?"

Jackson nodded.

"Any chance we can take Adam into custody without the Alliance finding out?" Dillard paused. "If we could do that, we might have a chance to nail more members of the group."

Tom smiled and said, "I have an idea that might work."

"How's that?" Dillard asked.

Tom chuckled. "How do you feel about telling a few lies?"

"You're kidding me," Connor said, reading from the script Tom Heeter had given him. "The FBI really has their hands on a CD intended for the Delphi Alliance?"

Tom and Connor were seated at Connor's breakfast table, each reading from prepared scripts. Careful checking of the device used to bug Connor's apartment showed it was still working. Hopefully an Alliance member was listening.

"I can't tell you how we came by it," Tom answered, "at least not yet, but I have it with me if you'd like to listen to it. Can we use your CD player?"

"We could if the power was on."

"Peoples Power will soon tap into Western's power grid so most areas of the city will have power again by tonight. With all your new locks I could leave this CD with you." Tom read that line with hesitation. "As soon as the power's back, give it a listen. Then get it back to me. I need to return it to the safe before someone misses it."

"Can I put this in my column tomorrow?" Connor read.

"I can't let you go that far. But by the time your book is finished, detailing the activities of the Alliance and how the FBI spoiled their plans time after time, I'm sure you'll be allowed to release details."

"Okay, let's see the CD," Connor said.

"Oops," Tom said, still reading from his script.

"Watch out! You almost dropped it!" Connor smiled at Tom; no CD had changed hands.

"Guard it with your life, Connor."

"Okay. It'll be safe in my CD player," Connor continued. "I need to head to work now. Hopefully, when I get home tonight, the power will be restored. I'll take notes for the book, and then return the CD to you. Will that work?"

"Only if you promise never to reveal who supplied you with this information."

"I promise." Connor winked. "Thanks, Tom. With your help, I'll have a best seller." Connor paused, before he read, "Wow! Look at the time. I'd better get to work. I hope the *News Telegrapher* has power."

Tom said, "Don't forget to lock up. That's a very important CD you've got. I didn't even take time to make a copy."

"See you tonight," Connor said, handing Tom his copy of the script as he left the apartment, headed to work.

Behind him Tom deactivated the listening device and opened the door to other FBI agents as they gathered in Connor's apartment to see if the trap they'd just set would catch anyone.

At the other end of the Alliance's listening device, Adam sat in shock. Another CD? One that should have come to him and the Alliance through Mario? If only there was a way to check with Mario to make sure another CD was really expected.

He hurried to the magnetic sign lot to get his van. If the redheaded man was at work, the apartment would be empty. Already congratulating himself on becoming a hero, Adam put on his uniform and headed for Connor's apartment.

When he arrived he strapped on his tool belt and entered the building. He passed a maid mopping floors, and continued on to Connor's door. With a key from his pocket, he unlocked the door and hurried into the apartment. He knew right where the CD player was kept.

"Looking for something?" The voice was close to Adam's ear. He whirled, reaching for the door knob, but his hands were jerked behind him. "Search him," Buford said handcuffing Adam.

"He came alone," reported Tom, removing his disguise as a maid. He reached into Adam's pockets. "Got it." He held up the key to the white van's ignition, then whispered into his two-way radio, "Send the medics and bring the uniform."

"You cannot hold me," Adam blustered. "You cannot arrest me. I did nothing wrong."

"I don't believe anyone said a word about arresting you, Adam, even though you broke into this apartment just now. It isn't our intent to *arrest* you. We have other plans for you. Some you won't like."

"I need water," Adam said as two men in EMT attire entered the room with a stretcher. One of them carried a white uniform.

"Have a seat," said one of the fake medics, reaching out to take Adam's arm.

"No." Adam pulled away, but stumbled. His head hit the floor, knocking him unconscious.

He was placed on the stretcher, and covered with blankets. A few minutes later he was loaded into a waiting ambulance.

"Are you ready?" Buford asked. Tom had changed from dirty coveralls to a clean white uniform that said *Thompson's* on one pocket.

"Let's do it," Tom replied, picking up Adam's tool belt and donning a wig of short black curls.

When the men left Connor's apartment Buford got into his car and Tom, in his disguise as Adam, entered the white van.

CHAPTER
25

It was noon when two FBI agents, wearing what passed for Whittington police uniforms, stopped at the door to apartment 312 on Kentucky Avenue. Their knock was answered by a female in a smock.

"Yes?" she asked softly.

"Mrs. Bailey? Mrs. Adam Bailey?" It was Tom Heeter asking the question.

The woman stepped back and pushed against the door to close it.

"You don't understand." Buford Jackson planted his foot firmly in the door's opening. "Your husband has been in an accident. Do you understand? *Traffic accident? Crash?*"

The woman nodded slowly, clinging to the door frame. "Adam?" she whispered.

"There was an accident. A crash. A white van was hit by a big truck. It has taken a long time to remove the injured man. We had trouble learning his name." Buford showed her a picture in which Tom, dressed as Adam, appeared badly hurt.

Tears filled the woman's eyes.

"We are sorry to bring bad news, but...," Tom left the sentence unfinished. He fiddled nervously with a button on the jacket of his blue uniform—a button that was actually a miniature camera.

"I must see Adam," the woman said. She crossed her arms in front of her chest as if to ward off evil.

"He is dead." Buford's response was a soft whisper.

"You must take me to him," the woman said.

"There was a fire," Tom interjected, embellishing the lie.

The distraught woman bowed her head. "I must see my Adam. I must take him home."

"We'll arrange things as quickly as we can with immigration or whoever else needs to be contacted. Will you be all right? Do you have friends who can stay with you?"

Yolinda Bailey nodded and pushed to close the door, but not before an unmistakable profile was evident. If all went well, the button on Tom's uniform would have a great shot of the very pregnant Mrs. Bailey.

"Now then, Adam," Dillard said to the cowering young man seated across from him. "Let's talk about where you were last night."

"You cannot prove my being gone," Adam said, so upset he'd forgotten a more correct form of English. "My countrymen have double happiness at happenings of the night. I wish I might have been part of it."

"What happens if we contact the Immigration and Naturalization Service? Does INS have any record of your entry into this country?"

"I am student with visa."

"Of course you are. How many years ago was the visa issued? Which academic program are you enrolled in? Are you still a full time student as required by your F-1 visa? Might INS or the US Department of State consider you guilty of terrorist-related activities and ask us to take over for them?"

"I have driver's card and secret security number."

"Do you mean *social* security number?"

"I need water."

"You get nothing until you answer some questions. Is it true the man you call Mario has returned to your country, or," Dillard smiled, "maybe it was just a way to leave you holding the bag?"

Adam looked confused.

"Another thing you might consider," Dillard continued, "is whether Mario was called home, or whether we set that up so we could grab him at the airport. Maybe he's in a cell because he violated his visa requirements."

Adam put his head in his hands.

Hoping the man was about to crack, Dillard added, "and what about your wife?" Dillard turned over a photograph taken with the aid of Tom's button camera. The picture had been upside down on the table, between the two men. Dillard admired it for several minutes before turning it around and pushing it across the table toward Adam. "Your wife's a real knockout, as we say in this country."

Adam scowled at the man across from him. "Our happiness is great! To die for our homeland is a great honor."

Dillard waited for a quick count to five before speaking. "And will it be a great honor for your son, who has not yet been born, to die for a country he has never known?"

Adam looked startled.

"You are probably aware that we've checked through the briefcase you had in the van. We've found an interesting dart that I suspect will contain the same rare poison used to murder Agent Morgan. I suggest you give some thought to what awaits you at the hands of Sam's friends and business acquaintances." Dillard nodded at the guards who had escorted Adam to the interrogation room. On cue they stepped forward. Dillard pushed back his chair and stood. "I guess I'll leave you to them, Adam." He left the room.

"Learn anything?" Tom asked as he and Dillard passed in the hall.

"Not yet. I'm putting him on suicide watch. He keeps asking for a drink and I'm concerned that we didn't search him as thoroughly as we should have."

###

Teddy and Thelma sat close to the windows, working half-heartedly in the dim, chilly office. The hands of the battery-operated clock on the wall seemed to move slowly. Outside, the weak October sunshine promised minimal respite from the effects of the power outage. Unable to use computers, the women were addressing envelopes by hand.

The phone rang, and Thelma grabbed it. "Girl Friday," she greeted, then listened a moment. Suddenly she gasped. "I'll meet you in front of the building." She slammed the receiver in its cradle and jumped to her feet.

Teddy looked up. "What's wrong?"

Thelma said, "M–my b–boys. There's been an accident. I must leave. My husband is picking me up to take me to the hospital." Her face muscles were twitching as she struggled to get her coat on. What her husband had really said was, "get the hell out of Dodge. They're on to us."

"Are both twins in the hospital?"

"I've got to leave," Thelma said.

Teddy added, "Let me know how the boys are, or if you'll be in tomorrow."

With a nod, Thelma bolted for the door.

Teddy shook her head, but continued working. It wasn't until lunchtime that she discovered Thelma's purse on the floor. In her hurry to leave, Thelma had left it behind. Teddy moved to the file cabinet to get Thelma's employment file to call about her purse. She opened the slim brown folder in which she'd filed the form, and found it empty. For a moment she stared at the folder, her mind stalled. Where was Thelma's application form?

A quick search of other folders and other locations didn't turn it up. Thelma would need her driver's license and her house keys, but how to get them to her? When Teddy couldn't find a telephone number in the phone book, she called information and learned Rasmussen's number was unlisted.

Still hoping for a phone number, Teddy opened Thelma's purse and found a small purple address book. Thelma's name, address and phone number were on the inside cover. Propping the book open on her desk, Teddy dialed and waited. No one answered. Thelma hadn't mentioned which hospital her boys were in so tracking her down that way wouldn't work.

Teddy waited a few minutes before calling Thelma's number again.

"Yes?" answered the out-of-breath woman.

"Thelma! It's Teddy. You forgot your purse. Will you need it?" Teddy imagined Thelma's look of panic as one more problem surfaced.

"Yes! I've been looking for it, but I can't leave. I'm at home with Cole and my husband is at the hospital at Cameron's bedside." There was a pause. Thelma was still breathing hard. "It's asking a lot, but could you bring my purse here? It would certainly help."

Teddy considered the possibility. Could she risk going to the home of an Alliance member? Would it be any more dangerous for her to be with Thelma at her home, than it was being with her in the office? With Bob Rasmussen at the hospital, she should be safe dropping off the purse if she left before he returned.

"Please help us," Thelma said.

"Why don't I put your purse in your mailbox? Then if you have to leave before I get there, it'll be safe."

"Thank you." Thelma sounded relieved. "I live at 2020 Lincoln Street."

"I'll bring it as soon as I can," Teddy said, hanging up. She grabbed her purse and Thelma's, and headed down the staircase beside her office.

"Stop her," Dillard yelled. He'd been taking his turn wearing the earphones connecting him to Teddy's telephone.

Tom looked up. "Stop who?" he asked.

"Sanderson. She's on her way to the Rasmussen's."

"She wouldn't risk going there," Tom said, with a laugh. "She's uneasy just having Thelma in her office."

"We didn't tell her they had no children. *They've* told her their boys were in some kind of accident and they asked Sanderson to bring Rasmussen's purse to her. Teddy's headed there now."

"My God," Tom exclaimed. "That's Lincoln, isn't it? 2020?" At Dillard's nod, Tom flew out the door.

On Lincoln Street Teddy pulled up in front of a tan two-story house with a green door. The shades were drawn and the house looked deserted. She had parked in front of Thelma's mailbox, but it was on the passenger side of her car. Quickly she left her car and ran to the mailbox to deposit the purse. A screech of brakes startled her.

Jammed against the front of her car was a gold Cadillac containing the man who'd pretended to be Donald Kennedy. Teddy rushed behind her car to reach the driver's side and slipped into the seat. Before she could shut the door Bob grabbed her arm and pulled her out.

"Nice to see you, Miz Sanderson," he said, gripping her firmly. "Thelma," he called to the woman joining them. "Put our car in the driveway." Raz picked Teddy up with his beefy arms and carried her, kicking and screaming, into the Rasmussen house. A moment later, Thelma joined them.

Bob shouted, "Grab her keys, and get her car out of sight."

Thelma reached for the car keys in Teddy's hand, but Teddy's self-defense training kicked into gear, and she used them to stab Thelma. At the same time she slammed her foot down on Bob Rasmussen's big right foot.

Bob howled in pain, shoving Teddy hard against the wall. Stunned and off balance, she was slow to react. His meaty hand caught her jaw, slamming her head against the wall again. This time Teddy sank to the floor, unconscious.

"That should hold her for a while." Bob reached down to rub his throbbing foot. He barked at Thelma, "Get rid of her car!"

Tom Heeter arrived at 2020 Lincoln just as Teddy's Corolla was pulling out of sight further up the block. He put his foot firmly on the gas and tried to catch up. A big yellow school bus turned the corner onto Lincoln blocking his view of the little Corolla. He slapped his steering wheel in frustration and grabbed his cell phone to call Teddy, but she didn't answer.

Tom called Dillard. "I'm trying to follow Teddy's car," he reported, "but traffic is heavy. Hopefully she's headed back to her office. Watch for her arrival and let me know."

When Tom finally pulled into the parking garage at the Stettler, he noted Teddy's car in her assigned space. He raced up the stairs to her office. It was time she learned that Rasmussens had no children.

Unfortunately her office door was locked and no one answered. He hurried to Dillard's office. "Teddy's office is locked, but her car's downstairs. Where is she?"

Dillard said, "No one's been in her office. I didn't even know her car had returned."

Tom replied, "Either she's running errands, or someone else drove her car."

Dillard grabbed his phone. "I'll put out a *be on the lookout* for her."

Tom said, "I'll search her office. Maybe I can find something there to aid in the *BOLO.*"

It was late afternoon when Tom knocked on the Rasmussen's front door. An examination of Teddy's office hadn't produced any reason for her leaving, except to deliver Thelma's purse to her. He pounded on the green door for the second time, and finally Thelma answered.

"Hi, Tom," she said. "What are you doing here?"

"I know Teddy was bringing your purse to you and I'm making sure she did."

"I've got it right here," Thelma answered. "She left it in the mailbox for me."

"And how are your twins, Thelma?" Tom asked, just as a voice behind Thelma spoke up.

"What's going on?" asked the man joining them. "Why isn't my dinner ready, Thelma?" Bob Rasmussen roughly pulled his wife away from the door. "Fix my dinner," he glowered, then turned to Tom. "We aren't buying whatever you're selling." He slammed the door shut.

It was an evening news story about a traffic accident that caught Myron's attention. The burned vehicle was reported to have been a white truck with the name *Thompson* on the side. According to the newscaster, authorities were unable to locate an employer by that name.

Myron slammed his beer bottle on the table. *Hot Damn! The little prick went ahead with his eco-terrorist plans, but he's screwed up and gotten himself killed. He won't be able to get rid of Teddy for me. I should have known he'd foul up.* Myron studied his watch, figuring how many hours he had until his appointment with Gwen Morgan. He needed a backup plan. He polished off his beer, and made a few notes, his pencil tapping nervously as he considered his dilemma with the approaching deadline.

He looked at the business card given him by the man at the magnetic sign shop. Was he one of the terrorists? It looked like a visit to the tan house with the green door was in order. Whoever lived there was as guilty as Adam had been. Maybe he could be blackmailed into ending Teddy's life and meeting Myron's deadline in—he glanced again at his watch—in about twenty hours.

Power was gradually restored to the core of the city and emergency services were up and running. William Smith and the power plant's Board of Directors were meeting to get a handle on all the problems. Utility crews were working around the clock, with some on standby in case of additional attacks. As one commentator dryly put it, "This has been a test of our emergency alert system."

Viewers were not impressed with the so-called *test*. Restoration of services was what they wanted. Complaints from frustrated citizens were being handled as best they could. The question most often asked seemed to be: *How could elected officials have allowed such a thing to happen?*

In the Stettler Building, one office remained closed and locked, even though the power had been restored to the building. Teddy Sanderson, Girl Friday, was, according to her answering machine, unavailable.

Tom Heeter had been up all night. He was eager to hear the details of the interrogations of Adam Bailey but he needed to find Teddy first. He hurried into Dillard's office. The senior agent was on the telephone, motioning impatiently at Tom to take a seat as he continued his conversation.

"No answer at her house either?" He stared at Tom as he spoke. "How about her car? Is it still in the basement? Can we get fingerprints" He rubbed his eyes wearily with one hand. "Okay, keep looking. Check the Rasmussen residence, and the Bailey apartment. And you might as well contact Connor Douglas while you're at it. But don't tell that hothead why you're curious. I suppose you better find out what her ex-husband's been doing lately."

Brighton shook his head and frowned at Tom. "Okay, okay!" He was nearly shouting. "Keep me informed. And check with her friends. What's their name? Ravensworth? Yeah. That's right. Check with them."

Brighton slammed the receiver in its cradle and looked at the young agent sitting across from him. "We've dropped the ball," he said. "Sanderson's gone missing."

CHAPTER
26

Teddy Sanderson inhaled stale air as she sat tied to a small wooden chair. Her head ached and she had a bad taste in her mouth.

I must be in a closet, she thought, her heart racing. She hated small spaces. An unknown number of hours earlier, Bob Rasmussen had carried her into his house and struck her at least once. When she came to, she'd found herself gagged, blindfolded, and being thrust into the trunk of a car that smelled like sweaty gym clothes. Where had they taken her? Where was she now?

She could hear voices in another room, but she couldn't understand what they were saying. Were they talking about her? What did they intend to do with her?

The FBI's listening equipment in her office would have recorded her plan to take Thelma's purse to her. But if she was no longer at the Rasmussen's house, what would guide Tom to this location? Teddy slumped against the uncomfortable chair and tried to make plans. She should have been smarter about helping an Alliance member, instead of walking into a trap.

Myron knocked again on the green door of the tan house. When no one answered, he considered kicking the door down. He didn't know how eco-terrorists operated. Did they blow up something, then leave town until things cooled down? He looked at the neighborhood around him. Kicking in a door wouldn't be quiet and being in jail for breaking and entering wouldn't help him find a new hit man to meet his deadline.

He considered Adam's residence on Kentucky Avenue. If Adam had been the Alliance's ringleader and the FBI hadn't caught on to that, searching his apartment might turn up names of people he worked with.

Myron hurried back to his car. Time was growing short and he'd just wasted another hour. He started his car, fighting the impulse to drive carelessly. There was no point spending time talking to cops. He glanced in the rear view mirror, then, as if he had all the time in the world, he pulled into traffic and slowly headed for Kentucky Avenue and apartment 312.

###

A flurry of activity was taking place in Dillard's office. Special agents and representatives from key agencies were exchanging information as they searched for Teddy Sanderson. The question being asked was whether her absence was due to the Alliance or to her recently paroled ex-husband. Tom had found the purple address book propped open on Teddy's desk. He'd paged through it, noting stars beside the listing for *Computerized Signs*. Could that be an Alliance conspirator? Would it lead him to Teddy?

He copied the book's pages and gave them to Dillard to check against various locations for which they now had telephone numbers, thanks to Thelma's phone calls. Soon they might be able to solve problems created by the purple book's use of coded names and phone numbers.

If Teddy gave Thelma her purse and Tom arrived in time to see Teddy's car drive away, had she been at the wheel, or was someone else driving? Who returned her car to the Stettler Building?

Tom's cell phone vibrated. "Heeter," he snapped.

"Buford here. We did a quick inspection of Sanderson's car. There's blood on the steering wheel. We sent samples to the lab along with some of Sanderson's hair. They'll check DNA. Did you find anything in her office that will help us?"

"I'll fill you in when I pick you up. I'm headed downstairs now. Be ready to leave."

Tom hurried to the parking garage, sorting various plans in his head. Armed with search warrants, he and Buford could stop at the Rasmussen house and make arrests. After that, they'd head for the address listed beside *Computerized Signs*.

Connor Douglas opened his door that morning to a burly FBI agent motioning him down the stairs. When they were outside, the agent said, "When did you last see Ms. Sanderson?"

"Let me think." Connor pushed fingers through his hair, his suspicions aroused. "It was the other day in Brighton's office. I don't think I've seen her since." He tried to read the expression on the agent's face. "Is something wrong?" His reporter's intuition was on alert, "Is she missing?"

"We'd just like to talk to her," the agent answered smoothly. "We thought you might be of help."

"I suppose you've tried her office?" Connor fished for information. "She has a secretary who ought to be helpful. I imagine she keeps close tabs on Teddy's whereabouts."

"Thanks for the suggestion." The agent headed toward his car.

"What's going on?" Connor called after him.

The agent turned and took a few steps back. "If you hear from her, let me know right away." He reached in his jacket pocket and pulled out a business card that he handed to Connor. "I pick up anytime. Just call."

"I'll do that." Connor studied the card, already planning what *he'd* do next. He returned to his apartment and closed the door. If Teddy had disappeared, what did that mean? He began punching numbers on his cell phone. "This is Connor Douglas, put me through to Tom Heeter."

The receptionist on the other end of the line was polite and businesslike. "One moment, sir." Connor waited for what seemed like a long time. What was taking so long?

Finally, the voice returned. "I'm sorry, sir. Mr. Heeter stepped out of the office and is unavailable at the moment. May I take a message?"

"Tell him Connor Douglas needs to speak to him about a very important matter. He has my number." Connor's smile was a tight grimace. That should jar Tom Heeter into responding. With his phone in his pocket, Connor slipped his flip flops on and headed for his car.

Tom and Buford arrived at the Rasmussen residence. "When I was here yesterday," Tom said, "Teddy was driving away. At least her car was driving away. I just assumed she was at the wheel."

"Stop beating yourself up," Buford advised. "Let's see what we can find here. If we're able to rule out the Alliance holding Teddy, then we'll need to have a serious talk with her former husband."

Tom nodded. "Let's go."

With guns drawn, the agents pushed through the Rasmussen's doorway, yelling, "FBI." Together they raced through the house checking rooms, closets, and any other hiding places.

"No one's here," Tom admitted, putting his gun away and putting on gloves. "Let's see what they left behind."

"I saw some documents in the dining room. I'll check those out." Buford hurried to the dining room table and began taking pictures of what he found there. "I think these are diagrams of that power plant they blew up."

Tom's eyes swept the living room searching for anything that would signal Teddy's presence in the house. "Thelma told Teddy her kids were hurt and she needed her purse delivered. She made it sound like her husband was at the hospital with one of the kids."

"And Teddy bought it?" Buford continued photographing papers. "You know Teddy better than anyone else. Would she deliver the purse? To the door of an Alliance kingpin?"

"She was going to put Thelma's purse in her mailbox. I don't think the subject of Rasmussen's children ever came up in briefings that included Teddy." Tom scanned the room as he spoke. When he spotted a roll of electrician's tape on the floor, he photographed it, and then bent to pick it up. "I have what looks like a blood stain on the carpeting under this tape. It's dry, but there's also what looks like blood on the tape." He dropped the tape in an evidence bag, and then lay a ruler beside the stain on the carpet. He took a picture, and pulled a swab from his pocket. He removed it from its sterile enclosure and dabbed at the stain before returning the swab to the enclosure.

Buford stepped around Tom to look at the stained carpet and his shoe snagged something near the desk. "Look at this," he said. "That woman left her purse even after Teddy dropped it off." His camera flashed, then he pulled a black tote from under the desk.

Tom looked at what Buford held. "No way," he said "That's Teddy's." They stared at each other.

"Blood *and* Teddy's purse? It looks like the Alliance has her." Buford headed for the door. "Call Dillard. Tell him to get forensics over here while you and I head for that starred address." As they rushed to their car, Buford added, "Why would the Alliance kidnap Teddy?"

"Rasmussen knows we're on to him as an Alliance member, and Teddy can connect him to Don Kennedy's murder."

"Looks like we can rule out her ex-husband as her kidnapper," Buford said.

Tom wasn't listening. He was punching Dillard's number. "Alliance members will be in hiding," he said. He could feel his stomach knotting. "Now that they've claimed responsibility for the death at the Peoples Power Plant, there'll be murder charges involved."

Buford said, "Tell Dillard to check Rasmussen's phone records. Maybe we can find out who he contacted after nabbing our girl."

Myron pounded on the door of apartment 312. When it opened, a pregnant woman in a maternity dress stood in the doorway. She had long black hair encircling one blond swatch that looped across the top of her head.

"Mrs. Bailey?" asked Myron. When she nodded he continued, "Do you understand English?"

She nodded again.

"I need to talk to the men your husband worked with. Can you tell me how to get in touch with them?"

"I do not know Adam's friends, and now my Adam has died. Your government has told me so." Tears filled her eyes.

"Don't you know the name of anyone Adam worked with?"

The woman shook her head and pushed the door shut.

Myron heard the lock snap into place. What now? With Adam dead, he needed to rethink his plans for Teddy.

CHAPTER
27

The FBI was arresting those for whom they had warrants, and the state police were searching for Rasmussen's missing car.

No one had brought Connor up-to-date on happenings, so when he considered how his apartment had first been searched by someone carrying a pizza, he decided to see if a pizza would get him into Adam's apartment. When he arrived at apartment 312, he was carrying a large pizza. He was unaware of Myron Ratini parked nearby, trying to figure out what *his* next move would be.

Heart thumping under his jacket, Connor knocked on 312 and called out, "Pizza delivery." If no one answered the door, he'd eat the pizza himself.

"Yes?" An earthy-looking woman stood before him, her straight hair pulled into a limp, gray pony tail, her pale face stark and angular. One hand was bandaged. "We didn't order pizza," she said. She looked surprised when Connor popped open the lid of the pizza box to show a mouthwatering assortment of fragrant meats and cheeses.

Connor groaned. "Oh, no! I can't tell my boss I made another delivery mistake. He'll fire me for sure this time."

Thelma's mouth was watering. "I-I wouldn't want you to get fired," she said as her stomach growled out loud. She grabbed the purse Teddy returned to her, and shelled out money.

"Thanks, Lady," Connor said, pocketing the cash and noting the generous tip. "I'm naming my first kid after you, if you'll tell me your name." He winked at her, smiling flirtatiously.

Thelma laughed. "No one names babies Thelma anymore." She beamed at Connor as he turned to leave.

Delighted that he had a new piece of information, he returned to his car. Once more he tried to reach Tom Heeter.

"Heeter," answered the familiar voice.

Before Connor could respond, the door to apartment 312 opened. The woman named Thelma walked out carrying the pizza and a suitcase. Beside her was another lady, wearing a long gown.

"Can't talk, Tom," Connor blurted. "I'm at the apartment. You know, 312! I just delivered pizza to a lady named Thelma. She's leaving now. Getting into an old Cadillac with some foxy-looking babe. I'm going to follow them. I'll get back to you as soon as I can."

"Connor," shouted Tom into the dead phone. "Damn it, Buford." Tom turned to the agent behind the wheel of their car. "Head back to Rasmussen's. Connor's following Thelma and there's a good chance she's headed home."

The Alliance's captive had been given water and little else. She was hungry and her stomach growled.

"Tom, where are you?" she whispered. The tape had finally been removed from her mouth so she could at least lick her lips to moisten them. When the spicy aroma of pizza reached her, she thought there was no other smell as welcome. "Please," she whispered. "Let me have something to eat."

The women Connor followed took suitcases and the pizza inside the brown house near the corner of Westchester and Seventh. Connor called Tom to tell him, but added, "I'm going to look around, peek in windows. That sort of thing. Teddy might be in there. I'll let you know as soon as I discover anything."

162

"No, Connor. Don't do that. Those guys play for keeps. I'll be there with backup in ten, maybe twelve minutes."

"Can't wait that long," Connor replied. "I'm going to take a little stroll now."

Tom yelled, "No" but was cut off when the connection ended. "Damn it, Buford," Tom said. "Head for Seventh and Westchester. Connor and at least one of the Rasmussens is at the address listed beside one of the starred addresses in Thelma's purple book."

"Make up your mind, Tom. We're almost back at the Rasmussen house." Buford hung a sharp left and they headed for Seventh and Westchester. "What's going on?"

"The Rasmussens are on the move and that idiot reporter's following them. He's going to make matters worse."

At Seventh and Westchester Connor got out of his car and removed his jacket. He left his cap on, fluffed his long, stringy hair, and started slowly down the driveway next door to the brown house.

"What y'all doin' skulkin' 'round on my property?"

The question startled Connor. "You scared the crap out of me," he responded in an angry whisper. He could feel his heart racing as he turned to see who had spoken.

"That din't answer my question none," said the old man behind him. A rifle of some kind rested in one hand.

"Easy with that firearm," Connor whispered, searching for something believable to say. "I have credentials. Let me get them out. And lower your voice please!"

"No need to show cree-dentials if'n you gimme the reason yur creeping 'round on my land. You a tax man?"

"I'm not here about taxes. Are you Chad Mathews?" Connor made up the name, hoping there wasn't a real person by that name anywhere west of the Mississippi River.

"Never heard-a him."

"He's one of the men responsible for the explosion at Peoples Power," Connor invented.

"Well, I ain't him."

"Perfect," Connor breathed, relaxing for the first time in several minutes. "I've been following one of those terrorists we've been hearing about on the news." He spoke in a low voice, hoping to appeal to the man's prejudices. "That terrorist lady and her friend just went into the house next to yours." Connor pointed at the brown house. "I was thinking I might peek in a few windows to see what they're up to."

"That's Lyle Bascom's place. Don't hold much with his political views, but him and his missus are good folks. His wife just had a baby. That lady you followed might be a nurse since I know they been lookin' fir one."

"Do you know if the Bascoms have other visitors? Maybe a slender blond woman?"

"Wouldn't know. You want me to ask 'em?"

"No. Oh no. Please don't do that. If you don't mind, I think I'll just stick to my plan and look in a couple of windows."

"We don't let no hippie perverts into our neighborhood to snoop in our winders, young feller. So I'd guess 'lessen you march up to that there door and knock on it real hard-like, you'll be gittin' back in your V-hicle and moseying on down the road."

Connor looked hesitant.

"In fact," the gun was now pointed at Connor. "I think y'all knockin' on that there door is jest what's happenin' next. Git movin'."

Without another choice, Connor slowly made his way to the door of the brown house. He knocked softly.

"Give it a good solid thump." The main encouragement came in the form of the gun barrel sharply nudging Connor's back.

Connor winced and knocked harder. When the door opened, Lyle Bascom stood in the doorway. "What's going on, Clyde?" he asked. "Why're you and Ole Betsy bringing me a stranger?"

"Caught this here hippie pervert set to look in your winders. Probably set on watchin' yur missus breastfeed the young'n. What'cha want me to do with him?"

"Who are you?" Lyle asked Connor.

"I–I," Connor couldn't find any words. "I just sold a pizza to a lady and I thought if she had a large crowd to feed, I could make another sale." Connor shrugged his shoulders helplessly.

"So you followed her here? You must have lots of time on your hands." Lyle gave Connor a curious look. "I don't believe you for a minute, kid. Thanks for being vigilant, Clyde," he congratulated his neighbor. "I'll handle this now." He grabbed Connor's arm and roughly pulled him inside.

"Glad to hep out," Clyde said, turning to head home.

With Connor in their midst, Lyle asked, "Anyone know this guy?"

"That's the pizza man," Thelma volunteered. "What's he doing here?"

"Good question." Bob Rasmussen walked over to Connor. He grabbed his chin and tilted his head upward. "I remember you," he said, beginning to search Connor's pockets. "I met you outside of Sanderson's office. You tried to pass yourself off as FBI." Bob pulled a card out of Connor's pocket. "Press?" He eyed Connor suspiciously. "You're from the newspaper?"

Connor nodded, wishing he'd listened to Tom Heeter and waited.

"Looks like we got us an unwanted guest," Bob sneered, jerking Connor's hands behind him while Lyle tied a rope around Connor's wrists. "Get moving," Bob said, shoving Connor into a darkened room. They pushed him down on a wooden chair. "You got yourself a visitor, Sanderson. Say *howdy* to this nosey guy from the press." Bob gave a hollow laugh. "Thelma, get this jerk gagged."

"Connor?" Teddy whispered, perking up for the first time since her kidnapping. If he could find her Tom couldn't be far behind.

However, the person not far behind Connor had black curly hair and wanted Teddy dead. He'd seen the redhead enter the brown house with a gun at his back, but the gun toting neighbor had left the scene and the redhead hadn't.

Myron glanced at his watch. He still had time before he needed to meet with his parole officer. Even if he could find someone who'd take care of Teddy for him, she'd have one more week to live and he'd be stuck in Whittington until time for one more meeting with his parole agent. He picked up his cell phone to call Gwen Morgan. He'd tell her that due to some unforeseen problem he expected to be late for today's meeting.

CHAPTER
28

Buford Jackson and Tom Heeter were hurrying to the address Connor had given Tom. It matched the starred address in Thelma's purple address book and was listed in FBI files as the residence of Lyle and Susan Bascom.

The two agents were aware of procedures—keep it quiet, quick, and don't give suspects time to alert their buddies. A cadre of agents was speeding to the Bascom residence in unmarked cars to provide backup and seal off streets, while city police directed traffic away from the neighborhood. The authorities were trying to avoid media attention. The last thing they needed was television helicopters hovering over the house.

The plan was to remove people from their homes, thus securing the neighborhood. Bascom's house would then be surrounded from safe vantage points, including roof tops, if that was feasible. When all was ready, SWAT would storm the house, hoping to catch Alliance members off-guard long enough to rescue Teddy and Connor.

There was always the possibility of gunfire and Tom dreaded the situation if that happened. He gritted his teeth. He'd be glad when this day was over.

There had been no opportunity for Teddy and Connor to carry on a conversation. The minute Connor was thrust into the room Thelma taped his mouth shut and covered his eyes. Teddy stayed quiet during that procedure, hoping to escape being taped again. When they'd ripped it off of her earlier, it left tiny stinging cuts in her skin, especially when she licked her lips to ease their dryness. Once Connor was secure, Thelma left the room.

Teddy could hear the reporter struggling in his chair. She whispered, "Connor, did you come alone? Does Tom know where we are?"

His answer was a series of undistinguishable moans which Teddy couldn't interpret.

She whispered again, "Once for no and twice for yes. Does anyone know where we are?"

"This isn't a party." Bob Rasmussen's voice silenced the laughter in the room next to the hostages. "We need to decide what we're going to do with those two in the bedroom. Don't you people realize how bad things are? If we're caught...." He let the sentence hang, unfinished. "The way I see it," he continued, "we need to get out of here. Now!"

"Take those two with you," Lyle said. "You're not leaving them for me to deal with."

Bob continued. "If we take them along, we can dump them at the border, unless someone has a better suggestion?"

"If we dump them, and I'm not sure what you mean by that," Thelma said, "but if we did and if we were followed, the FBI would surround us as soon as we got rid of them. If we keep them for hostages, we have a better chance of getting away."

Lyle interrupted, "Whatever you decide, my wife and I are out of it. I have too much to lose to be part of any getaway plan. If the FBI comes here, I'll say you forced your way in. We've been friends for a long time, Raz, but that's the extent of our relationship. Is that clear?"

Bob said, "I'll need some money. You can help with that, can't you?"

"To a limited degree." Lyle nodded at his wife and she left the room. A few minutes later she returned and handed a fat envelope to her husband. He took out several bills, but as he attempted to hand them to Raz, the big man grabbed the fat envelope.

"You keep those bills," Raz said, nodding at the few bills in Lyle's hand. "When you get in touch with Alliance members, ask them to contribute some cash." He stuffed the envelope in his shirt pocket and turned to the women. "Gather your things, ladies. We're getting out of here. That reporter may have told someone where he was headed."

###

Teddy could hear increased activity in the room next door as people got out of their chairs and moved about. She whispered to Connor, "If they move us to a new location, Tom won't know for sure that we were ever here. Are you wearing your orange-checkered flip flops?"

Connor moaned twice.

"Kick one into the corner of the room, for Tom to find." There was the sound of a shoe hitting the wall just as the door opened.

Bob was saying, "Thelma, you women wrap a blanket around the girl and get her out of here. Put her in the Caddy's back seat, on the floor. I'll take care of the reporter."

Within minutes Thelma and Yolinda were sitting in the Cadillac with Teddy on the floor between them. She was still wrapped in a blanket, but her head was covered only by the women's skirts. Connor had been stuffed in the car's trunk. His head was jammed against a suitcase and his legs bent to fit his lanky frame into the remaining space. His blindfold was gone, but tape was still over his mouth.

Bob finished loading suitcases and got in the car, slamming the door, He winced as he pushed his injured right foot on the gas pedal. The car jerked backward. He nodded at Lyle, and steered the gold Cadillac down the street.

###

"Fancy that," Myron said from his hiding place in the Accord, parked beyond the Bascom's. Three adults had gotten into the car. In addition, two bundles that looked like trussed up bodies were also stuffed in it. Was Teddy already dead?

When the car left the driveway, only the three adults were visible. If luck was on Myron's side, two dead bodies would soon be dropped along a deserted stretch of highway. Still, he'd need to make sure the job was done right. He had two full hours before he was due to meet with his parole officer. If he hurried, he might be there on time.

Staying a respectable distance behind, Myron followed the gold car. In anticipation of what he hoped to find, he whistled a happy little tune.

Tom Heeter joined FBI agents in the Bascom neighborhood. They were getting ready to pounce. Agents had quickly and quietly knocked on doors, ordering residents to leave. The only protestor was the Bascom's neighbor, but after two agents pushed their way into Clyde's house, they finally convinced him they were special agents and not tax collectors or whiskey revenuers. The Bascom's car stood in their driveway while Connor's was parked down the block. No other vehicle was in sight.

After the agents secured the neighborhood, a SWAT team made its way to the front of the Bascom house. A moment later the door flew into the room, with agents holding guns entering right behind it. The startled Bascoms looked from the damaged door to the dark-clad figures spilling into their house.

Lyle jumped to his feet. "What's going on?" He paused at his wife's side.

"You're headed downtown, Mr. Bascom. We'll sort it out there. You, too, lady. Bring the kid and let's go." The agent who'd spoken nodded as team members spread out to search the house.

Susan Bascom turned to her husband. "Lyle, do something. We can't take the baby out. She's too little. The doctor said she shouldn't be outside in this weather."

He gave his wife a reassuring nod. "Stay calm. I'll handle this." He turned to the SWAT members. "I'm assuming your actions have something to do with Bob Rasmussen." He met the blank stares, then continued. "Bob stopped in a few minutes ago, asking for money because he's in some kind of jam. He's a long-time friend, so I gave him a few hundred. He thanked me and drove away. I didn't see who was with him, and I have no idea where he was headed."

"What direction did he take?" Tom Heeter had pushed his way to the front of the SWAT team.

"He left not five minutes ago, and was headed down the street to the north." Lyle glanced at his wife, but turned back to look at the agents. "Can't you leave us alone? That's all we know!"

At that moment an agent came in from the kitchen. "Lots of dirty plates in there for just two people," he announced, "and there's a big pizza carton!"

"Who had dinner with you, Bascom?" Tom asked, taking a step toward Lyle.

"Okay, so Bob and his wife were here long enough to share the pizza they brought along, but that's all. They were in a hurry!"

"Who was in a hurry, Lyle?" Tom asked. "How many?"

"Just Rasmussen, his wife and another woman, but I don't know anything about her since we weren't introduced."

"Describe her," Tom demanded.

"Dark hair. What may have been maternity clothes." Lyle looked up as another agent entered the room and tapped Tom's shoulder.

"It looks like two people were tied to chairs in a back bedroom, and we found this." Buford showed Tom a colorful flip flop.

"That's Connor's!" Tom exclaimed. "The two tied up must have been Teddy and Connor."

Buford nodded. "Dillard ordered a police bulletin for patrol cars to *be on the lookout* for Rasmussen's Cadillac."

"We must have missed them by minutes. Teddy's in more danger now than before." Tom shook his head and again wondered, *If I was Bob Rasmussen, what would I do next?*

CHAPTER
29

"Where are we going?" Thelma cradled Teddy's head against her leg. Yolinda hadn't spoken a word from the moment Thelma showed up to help her move.

Bob's voice was tight. "I haven't figured that out yet, but it's almost sunset. Once it gets dark, we'll have more choices."

"Won't the authorities be looking for this car?"

"That's exactly right," he agreed, then added, "I've got it! I know where we'll go."

In the rear view mirror close to Bob's head, Thelma could see a satisfied smile on his face. He obviously had a plan. She only hoped it didn't include murder.

"How's the girl doing?" Bob asked after he'd been driving for a while.

"Teddy or Adam's wife?"

"Your employer," Bob snapped.

"She's quiet. She knows not to give us any trouble."

"You got any of that electrician's tape back there?" Bob made a right turn onto a well-traveled road leading into an industrial park.

"Yes, there's some tape here."

"Well, put some on her mouth," Bob instructed. "And see if you can get some twisted around her legs."

Thelma pushed her skirts from Teddy's face.

"Thelma." Teddy mouthed the word in a whisper. "Let me go. Please."

Thelma glanced at Bob's face in the mirror, making sure he hadn't heard Teddy's plea. She knew if she crossed her husband he'd make her wish she hadn't. But, courts looked favorably on those who helped victims. If Teddy was alive and could testify, she could tell the courts who helped her.

"What's taking so long?" Bob shouted. "Get the job done!" He glanced in the mirror while keeping a watchful eye on the speedometer.

"It's hard to do in these cramped quarters," Thelma responded, nudging Yolinda. "Hold her legs while I tape them."

Yolinda held Teddy's legs, but again she had nothing to say.

"I'll be checking," Bob shouted. "You get her taped up good and tight, or you'll be sorry."

After Teddy's legs were bound, Thelma pulled off more tape. She looked at Teddy's frightened face and checked to see where Bob's attention was focused. Looking back at Teddy she winked then licked her lips and paused.

Teddy immediately licked her lips, leaving as much moisture as possible on the surface. With a brief nod, Thelma put the tape she was holding over Teddy's swollen mouth.

"Get her covered up," Bob instructed from the front seat. "We're coming into a busy area."

After they turned into long-term parking at the airport, he headed toward the farthest, darkest corner. When he found a space, he pulled into it and shut off the motor. "Wait here while I find some new wheels." He tossed the car keys to Thelma. "Unload the suitcases," he added as he left to walk down rows of parked cars.

"Get out," Thelma urged Yolinda as she opened her car door. She walked to the back of the car, and unlocked the trunk. The two women pulled suitcases out, ignoring Connor's moans. When they were finished Thelma slammed the lid back down, and returned to the car's back seat for the suitcase under Teddy. As she grabbed it, she pulled the blanket from around Teddy and pushed a tiny key into one of her bound hands.

At that moment Bob drove up in a van. He hustled Yolinda into the rear seat, then activated the Cadillac's child-protector locking-devices.

"I've got the ticket," Thelma called, waving the slip they'd received when the Cadillac entered the area. Bob returned to the van. A moment later he and the women drove away.

"I don't think they did a very good job," Myron mumbled, after observing the activity around the Cadillac. He had followed them for nearly an hour and they'd made no stops to dump dead bodies. Two bodies put into the car had to mean two were still in it, but were they dead or alive? Myron parked at a distance, prepared to check.

###

Tom Heeter was still wondering what Bob Rasmussen might do to elude the law. What was it bank robbers did as soon as they got the bank's money? That was easy. They drove a few blocks and switched cars so any witness who saw the getaway car would be handing out misleading descriptions of the vehicle.

If I was Bob Rasmussen, Tom reasoned, *I'd ditch that gold Caddy as soon as possible.* The Cadillac was too obvious. Did Bob have another car waiting somewhere? One he could use if law enforcement began closing in? Not likely, but he may have had friends. Tom looked at Lyle Bascom and his frightened wife. "Let's talk about cars," he said. "Did you have a second one that Rasmussen took?"

"No, we just have the one," Lyle said. "And it's still here."

"You know," Tom said quietly, "if you don't help us, you won't be seeing that baby of yours again until she's ready for social security."

The tears in Susan's eyes spilled. "Please Lyle, think of the baby. You're a father now." Her voice was soft and pleading.

"It's this way." Lyle glanced from his wife to Agent Heeter. He fidgeted in his chair. "I told Rasmussen I didn't want any part of whatever the Alliance had in mind. Susan had problems with this pregnancy and I wanted to be with her. I am in no way responsible for anything the Alliance has done recently. I've been with Susan day and night for a week, mostly at the hospital."

"Stick to the subject," Tom said. "We were talking about Rasmussen and cars."

"I told you, all I had to offer him was cash. Raz took it, then he and his wife and that other woman got in the Cadillac and left."

Tom stared at him. "You're leaving something out. What or who else did he put in that Cadillac?"

Lyle looked again at his wife and then at Tom. He swallowed. "Raz had two hostages." Lyle squirmed in his chair, not meeting Tom's eyes. "He's unpredictable. I don't know what he intends to do with them."

"Where would he get another car? Is there another 'best friend' who could supply money or transportation?"

"I don't know. I don't think so."

"Where could he get another car?" Tom asked again.

"I don't know. I really don't."

"Let's say," Tom persisted, "that you helped with the last Alliance fire bombing and you needed to shake the law. Has the group ever discussed ways of getting another set of wheels?"

"Only somewhat. We talked about parking in crowded malls and hot wiring something we found there."

"Or long-term parking," Tom whispered. He turned and headed for his car. As he sped toward the airport, he radioed Dillard. "I'm hoping we'll find that Cadillac in long-term parking at the airport. I'm headed there now. Send EMTs and backup."

Teddy had waited, listening for the sound of car doors slamming and of a car leaving. She was fairly certain the key Thelma pressed into her hand was for her handcuffs, but she couldn't get her hands at an angle that allowed her to use it. After a while, she gave up and scrunched around on the floor of the Cadillac. She was too low to reach the window. When she finally maneuvered herself into position, she pulled back her legs, then slammed them hard against the opposite car door. She was determined to keep up the noise until someone heard her and came to her rescue.

She could hear the sound of planes. Was the Cadillac sitting in the parking lot at the airport? Was it in long-term parking where people might not return for weeks? She kicked the door again.

What had they done with Connor? Was he in the trunk? She doubled up her legs and gave the car door another hard kick.

Thump, thump!

The sounds came from the back seat of the gold car as Myron approached it. He looked in and a wide smile made its way across his face. The thumping was his ex-wife. She was wrapped up like a Christmas present. What a package she made. And who would be able to say for sure that some member of the Alliance hadn't strangled her before he left? Her back was to Myron so she hadn't seen him yet, but he looked forward to that moment when she did. Quietly he tried the door handle. Locked.

A muffled noise came from the area of the trunk. Myron walked to the back of the car and found a key in the trunk's lock. He twisted it and lifted the lid. The gagged man inside seemed to be alive and well, just very uncomfortable. Myron left the trunk lid ajar but he took the key.

The tape across Teddy's mouth wasn't tight enough to cut her skin as it had earlier. She was thankful Thelma allowed her to moisten her lips before the tape was applied.

Teddy tried to sit up. If she could maneuver her body around, she might be able to open the door from the inside. Her hands were handcuffed behind her, but her fingers still worked. Slowly she edged her body into a more upright position, and then pushed until her back was against the door. She could feel the door handle with the top of her head, but she couldn't move it. Bob had probably locked all the doors and windows before he left, using the child safety lock button. Teddy settled back down and got ready to thump the door again.

At that moment, she heard a noise outside. She thumped the door. Could she make her predicament known and be rescued? Still thumping, she twisted her head, trying to see over her shoulder.

The face staring at her through the window wasn't Tom or even some curious stranger. Teddy's heart sank. Waving at her, his mouth twisted in an ugly grin was her ex-husband. Teddy's eyes opened wide and she shuddered. She'd gone right from the frying pan into the fire.

CHAPTER
30

The look of fear on Teddy's face was exactly the treat Myron had hoped for. "How're you doing, Babe?" he asked with a broad smile. "I bet you never thought we'd meet up like this."

He shoved the keys he'd found in the trunk into the car door, and when the lock clicked, he opened the door. "Sit up," he instructed the frightened woman sprawled across the floor of the back seat. He pushed her into an upright position and crawled in behind her. With his legs outstretched, he pulled her onto his lap. "Might as well get comfortable," he said, pulling the car door shut behind him. He leaned against it, enjoying Teddy's struggles.

"Well, let's get to it before you wear yourself out." He wrapped his fingers around her throat and began squeezing. "I think we can make this last a nice long time."

###

"There it is." Tom had driven up and down row after row of vehicles in long-term parking before spotting the gold Cadillac in a back corner. Even from a distance he could tell the trunk was open. He leaped from his car and ran to the gold vehicle. In the trunk, tied up like a steer at a rodeo, lay Connor. "Where's Teddy?" Tom asked, pulling at Connor's gag.

"Thump! Thump!" A noise came from inside the car. Tom didn't wait for Connor's reply, but stepped to the Cadillac's side door and looked in.

Teddy lay across the unconscious body of a man with curly black hair. Her mouth and legs were taped, and her arms appeared to be handcuffed behind her. She looked scared to death.

"It's okay, Teddy," Tom called out, opening the doors on his side of the car. He reached across the unconscious man to grasp Teddy's shoulders. Gently he pulled her from the back floor, and sat her on the edge of the front seat. He eased tape from one corner of her mouth, trying not to tear her skin.

A paramedic's truck came to an abrupt stop beside Tom's car and medics hurried over. "How about using your scissors here," Tom called, pointing to Teddy's taped legs. As the tape was being snipped, he asked, "Who's the guy in back? Is that Myron?"

Teddy nodded.

"Take over," Tom said to the paramedic. "Then see about the fellow in the trunk." He moved back to Myron and rolling him on his side, was able to put handcuffs on him. He turned back to Teddy. "That'll hold him."

"Key," Teddy whispered, pushing her tongue against the tape still stuck to her mouth.

"I've got one right here," Tom said, reaching in his pocket.

Teddy twisted her body to display her cuffed arms and wiggled the fist that held a small key.

"They left you with a key to your handcuffs?" Tom took the small piece of metal and unlocked the restraints. Teddy slowly exercised her aching arms, then reached for the tape on her mouth. Tom asked, "Do you need medical attention?"

She shook her head. "Connor?"

"We have him," Tom said. "He's got some bruises, but I think he'll be fine."

"Myron?" She pulled the last bit of tape from her face.

"He's handcuffed. What happened to him?"

She shivered. "Somehow he was able to unlock the car door and get in behind me. When he closed the door, he pulled me onto his lap and began strangling me. I put my feet against the opposite door, and then pushed back and upward, hard and fast." She paused to rub the top of her head. "My head clipped him under the chin, slamming his head against the door hard enough to knock him out."

"Good job." Tom examined her head with gentle fingers. "I suspect you'll have quite a lump for a few days," he said.

"I was afraid he'd come to before anyone found us."

Tom pulled her close, cradling her trembling body. "As soon as the paramedics check you over, we'll get you and Connor some food and water."

"How about some pizza?" she asked with a teasing smile.

Tom kissed her forehead. "I suspect Connor won't want pizza for a very long time."

Thelma turned to her husband. "How long do you think it'll take before someone finds Teddy and that pizza fellow?" They'd been driving north for hours. It had grown dark and at the moment, they were entering another busy city.

"Who knows," Bob answered, pulling into a service station. "We need gas. I'll fill up while you ladies make a pit stop. But be quick about it."

Thelma and Yolinda hurried to the women's restroom, and entered stalls. Thelma's coat caught on the door lock, distracting her, but she returned to the sink area first. "Hurry up," she called, washing her hands, and running damp fingers through her hair. She turned on the electronic dryer and yelled over the noise, "Come on, Yolinda. Get moving." The dryer turned off and Thelma waited restlessly before knocking on the door to Yolinda's stall. When she hit the door, it bounced open far enough for Thelma to see the stall was vacant.

Instead of Yolinda, a pile of dark clothes lay draped across the toilet tank. A black wig lay on top along with a belly wrap that would fake a pregnancy. Thelma stared at the abandoned disguise. "I'll be," she whispered, collecting the items. She banged open the other doors to empty stalls, then rushed outside, looking around frantically, wildly searching the dark lot for signs of the missing woman. Would she even recognize Yolinda without her disguise? She'd never really looked at Adam's wife, and certainly Yolinda hadn't said much or done anything to call attention to herself.

Catching sight of his wife, Bob called, "What's keeping you?" He was drinking a soda.

Thelma hurried to him, waving the black wig. "You're never going to believe this."

Teddy and Connor huddled in Tom's car as it sped to FBI headquarters for debriefing. "Drop me at the *News Telegrapher*," Connor said. "I need to get to a computer as fast as possible. I think I can still make today's deadline."

"You promised to clear your stories with Dillard first. Remember?"

Connor mumbled a response, his lips pursed.

"Connor! Right?" Tom called, louder this time.

"Sure, sure." The reporter spoke half-heartedly, crossing his fingers. "I'll give it to Dillard first."

"Your word?"

"Okay, my word." He slowly opened his fists and uncrossed his fingers.

After debriefing, Teddy went home to curl up in bed. Daylight was approaching, but she was too tired to care. She snuggled down in the soft blankets, pulled a fluffy pillow under her head, and closed her eyes. Knowing Tom was on the living room sofa, writing his report, gave her the feeling of security she craved. She immediately fell into an exhausted sleep.

When Tom finished his report he looked in on the sleeping woman, then stepped to her side, planted a soft kiss on her cheek and headed to the Stettler. He needed to hand in his report and go over details with his boss.

Dillard had been up all night, expecting news of the Rasmussens' capture, but he'd received none. He greeted Tom just as his phone rang. "Dillard here." He punched the speaker button.

"It's Buford. We have a report that Rasmussen and his wife were spotted in a Ford van heading north on I-5. At that time they were about a hundred and thirty miles from the border."

"When was this?" Dillard asked.

"Sometime after midnight," Buford replied. "They pulled into a truck stop for food and gas. The guy who filled their tank said there was only a man and a woman. The pregnant lady wasn't with them."

"We've got border guards and FBI agents waiting at the border," Dillard said. "Keep on it. Let me know when you get them. I want Adam's wife brought here immediately. She's the pregnant one. If Rasmussen left her behind some place, I want to know where. Check with service stations on I-5. See if you can figure out the last place she was seen."

"Got it. State police are watching for the stolen van Rasmussen's driving, in case he decides to stop before he reaches the border."

"Nice going," Dillard responded, breaking the connection.

When Teddy awoke she smelled coffee. The early afternoon sun was streaming in her windows, but she was still tired, too tired even for fresh coffee. A note from Tom said he'd turn in his report and be right back.

She padded back to her bed, knowing she could relax. Myron was back in custody, the Rasmussens would be stopped at the Canadian border, and Delphi Alliance members, including Wendell Green, were either in jail or soon would be. Life was almost back to normal. She closed the bedroom shades, curled up in her favorite position, and listened to the grandfather clock in the dining room chiming the hour. She fell asleep before the chiming ended. The house was quiet and in the bedroom flowered curtains and dark shades dimmed the waning sunshine.

###

At the city jail that afternoon, the booking officer checked Myron Ratini into a holding cell and handed his admittance papers to the officer at the front desk. He said, "You might tell the nurse to look in on Ratini. He was injured yesterday and came here directly from the emergency room."

"Look at this!" his buddy replied, scanning the papers. "Ratini's on parole from the State Pen. He was supposed to see his P.O. yesterday. I'd better give her a call."

Gwen Morgan signed in with the jail officer at the front desk. After clearance, she clipped the ID badge on her suit coat and made her way to the booking office.

"Thought I'd come over today since I was nearby. Thanks for notifying me that my guy is here." She frowned. "Why can't he stay out of trouble?" She was reading the report on Myron's activities.

"Yeah, well, I guess that's your problem and not ours," the jailer said.

"It's going to be Ratini's problem," she responded. "He knew the rules. Where can I meet with him?"

"Room five is free." The officer waved his hand in the air, indicating the hallway to the right.

Gwen picked up her briefcase and a copy of the arresting officer's report. "See you later," she said. "Have Ratini brought down any time." She headed briskly toward room five.

"You're not listening to me, Myron," Gwen said later. "You did it to yourself, and because of that, you'll be headed back to prison to complete your original sentence." She restlessly paced the floor on her side of the table that separated them. A guard walking down the hall looked in and waved at her.

"I didn't do anything wrong," Myron protested. "I was trying to save my ex-wife when she hit me. My hands must have fallen to her shoulders when I lost consciousness, but they were never wrapped around her throat intentionally."

Gwen shook her head and stuffed his report in her briefcase. "You did it to yourself," she repeated, ready to leave. She grabbed for her purse, and as she reached for it, her identification badge fell to the floor. She bent to retrieve it.

In a flash, Myron spun around the table and slammed Gwen's head with his fist. She collapsed on the floor as he reached under her side of the table where the door-release switch was located.

Hearing the commotion in room five, the guard in the hall drew his gun and rushed into the room, only to find Myron waiting for him. A powerful punch landed in the over-weight officer's midsection, and when he doubled over, Myron grabbed his gun.

"Don't shoot," the officer pleaded, hands in the air.

"Drag the lady to that corner." Myron indicated a corner where a radiator stood. "Now listen carefully," he said. "Good hearing makes for a long life. Understand?"

The officer nodded.

"Take your handcuffs and put one on the lady's wrist, hook the other end around that radiator pipe and attach it to your wrist. Now then, when I walk out of here tell me how much yelling you'll be doing."

"None. No yelling. No noise. You want me to count to a couple thousand before I call for help?"

When the booking officer investigated later, Myron was gone, the key to Gwen's car was gone, and so was the money she'd had in her handbag.

In the parole officer's car, Myron made a quick stop at Adam's vacant apartment where he found Yolinda's abandoned robes. Slipping one long robe over his head, he set out to finish what he'd dreamed about for four years.

CHAPTER

31

Lydia Plummer pushed her garbage cart to the curb for Monday's pickup. As she headed indoors, she turned in time to see a white car stopping at the curb in front of Teddy Sanderson's house. She stepped onto her porch, pausing to catch a glimpse of Teddy's visitor, but the driver was slow leaving the car and Lydia was getting cold. She moved into her kitchen to watch from her window. "Well, look at that!" she called to Burt. "It's a foreign woman stopping at Teddy's. Maybe our neighbor's finally getting some women friends." Lydia watched as the figure in a long black robe reached Teddy's front door and appeared to be admitted into the house.

###

Tom and Dillard finished reviewing the interrogation tapes of talks with Lyle and Susan Bascom. They had informed Lyle of his options if he cooperated and the likely consequences if he didn't. Given those choices, he began talking, and once he started, they couldn't shut him up.

By late afternoon, FBI and State Police were rounding up members of local cells.

While Lyle was naming names, Tom and Dillard headed for their cars, congratulating themselves on the likelihood of closing down the Delphi Alliance in their area of the state.

"How about a beer at that little place on the waterfront?" Dillard asked, getting out his car keys.

"Can't do it," Tom said, yawning. "I promised Teddy I'd check in when we finished. She may have something more for us about the Rasmussen bunch."

A buzz alerted Dillard, and he reached for his cell phone. "Brighton here." There was a brief silence and then he yelled, "Send them. Now." He turned to Tom. "Get to Teddy's. Her ex is loose. SWAT's on the way."

Tom took off running, car key in hand. He peeled out of the parking lot, and bounced over the curb and into the street. He careened onto the boulevard as flashing lights on the car's roof twirled red and blue, its siren screaming.

Once inside, Teddy's visitor put the purloined house key from under the doormat in a pocket, and looked around. A clock ticked somewhere, and pillows lay in disarray on the sofa. On the coffee table lay a note: *"You were sleeping soundly. I didn't want to wake you. I'll check in again after my meeting with Dillard. Tom"*

The visitor smiled, aware now of deep breathing in the next room. Tiptoeing to the doorway, the figure peered into the darkened room.

The woman sleeping on the bed was curled on her side, blond hair fanning out on the pillows. Her quiet visitor picked up a pillow, grasped it firmly, and moved to Teddy's side. With the pillow held high, the scarf covering the visitor's face slipped to one side, revealing the intruder's twisted scowl. Sensing movement beside her and expecting it to be Tom, Teddy slowly opened her eyes.

The figure at her bedside wasn't the man she was beginning to love, but the man she feared more than anyone else. Before she could react, Myron slammed the pillow on her face.

The first heart-stopping moment the pillow cut off her breath, Teddy woke completely. Until then she'd only regarded the figure beside her bed as part of a dream, but the suffocating pressure had her struggling. Strong arms held the pillow tightly against her face. She kicked and twisted from side to side, desperately pinching and clawing until she drew blood.

Myron howled with pain but hung on, pushing harder. He yelled, "Not this time, Babe. You're finished. You're not telling anyone anything more about me."

The pillow followed Teddy's movements as she thrashed about. As her efforts grew weaker, Myron gave a hysterical giggle.

Teddy was aware only of her need for air, not the muffled sound of her bedroom door slamming against the wall, or of Myron shouting, *Don't shoot*—a plea cut short by a figure tackling him to the floor. With the pressure released, Teddy pushed the pillow away, and lay weak and trembling, gasping for air.

"Take over," Tom yelled at a SWAT member, rising from the floor where he'd landed on Myron's back. An exhausted Teddy lay on the bed, sucking in deep breaths. "It's okay, Teddy," Tom said. "It's okay. Myron's in custody. He can't hurt you now." Tom gathered her in his arms, and held her close. "How many times do I need to rescue you?" he whispered in her hair as he kissed the top of her head.

"I thought you were the one keeping track," she said with a deep sigh.

"Oh, Teddy," he moaned.

The group who'd worked on shutting down the Delphi Alliance in Whittington gathered at a little waterfront café; a favorite with FBI agents. Dillard had just joined the group, looking more relaxed than usual. He seemed satisfied with the results of their efforts, even though loose ends still needed to be tied up. Lyle Bascom sat in jail awaiting trial, but because he'd cooperated with law enforcement, a plea deal was in the works. Myron, on the other hand, was being sent back to prison to complete his manslaughter sentence. Additional charges would be filed for his attempts on Teddy's life and his assault of his parole officer and the prison guard. Better yet, the Internal Revenue Service had located the evidence they needed and was getting set to take its pound of the Ratini flesh.

Connor handed Dillard a beer and reached for another one—his second. He couldn't stop smiling. He was flush with the success of reporting his front page stories taken up by national news services. He'd made every deadline the *News Telegrapher* set up.

Tom, exhausted by the recent ordeal, asked for a week off. It was rumored he'd be headed to Hawaii. He glanced at his boss. "Still nothing on Adam's wife?"

Dillard shook his head. "We heard from a trucker after Connor's story aired. He reported picking up a blond woman at a truck stop where we think Rasmussen stopped for gas. He said the woman spoke perfect English. He dropped her off in Portland. If that was Yolinda and she's from outside the States, she's probably found her way to L.A. where pockets of her countrymen are hiding out."

"You sound like you doubt her foreign status," Tom said.

"It's the strip of blond hair that bothers me," Dillard answered.

"What about the Rasmussens?" Teddy asked.

Dillard cleared his throat. "We didn't do so well there; at least not yet. If they crossed the border into Canada, then they had help."

Tom smiled. "They'll make a mistake eventually. With every federal agent in the country on the lookout, we'll get them."

Teddy glanced at Special Agent Tom Heeter and smiled. A trip to Hawaii was set for next week, and she'd be traveling there with her own personal body guard. He'd told her that guarding her was the best assignment he'd ever had, and he'd suggested the trip for two as a *follow up.*

Tom caught Teddy's smile and returned it. Their eyes held for a long minute before they looked away, but their smiles lingered.

THE END